This Migrant Earth

Rolando Hinojosa's Rendition in English of

Tomás Rivera's . . . *y no se lo tragó la tierra*

Arte Publico Press
Houston

This publication is made possible by grants from the Texas Commission on the Arts and from the National Endowment for the Arts, a federal agency.

Arte Publico Press
University of Houston
University Park
Houston, Texas 77004

ISBN 0-934770-55-7
LC 85-073354

Preface

In the Spring of 1985, my English 342 class (Life and Literature of the Southwest) read, among other material, works by George Sessions Perry, Fred Gipson, Larry McMurtry, as well as some articles on the Texas literary tradition. This last brought us to Tomás Rivera's . . . *y no se lo tragó la tierra.*

It's been a successful book, and now in its fifteenth year of publication, I thought it time to devote more work on it; toward this, I began to write not a translation but rather an English rendition of Rivera's seminal work which he had written in Spanish.

The book, then, belongs to Tomás, and it is dedicated to his favorite people: readers, as he said ". . . of those square objects we call books."

A further dedication. To Rory, whose memory spans more than a quarter of a century, and because I love him, and because he wanted to remember.

Other Works by Rolando Hinojosa

The Klail City Death Trip Series:
Estampas del Valle
Klail City y sus alrededores
Claros varones de Belken
Korean Love Songs
Mi querido Rafa
Rites and Witnesses
The Valley
Dear Rafe
Partners in Crime
Klail City

Bowed by the weight of centuries he leans
Upon his hoe and gazes on the ground
The emptiness of ages in his face,
And on his back the burden of the world.

Edwin Markham

This Migrant Earth

I

II

The Paling Time and the Fading Year

Lost, that was what that year was to him. Lost. And though he tried—time and again—to remember and to recover that lost year (for that's what he called it), he found it would melt away. The words, too, had failed him, and how he needed words to find that lost, wandering year.

It would usually begin within—or, as if in—a dream where he imagined himself wide awake only to find he was dreaming still. How could this be?

And then, as time went on, he couldn't decide—admit, perhaps—tell, even—whether those things he thought on were real or not. Nor, could he swear that he had merely dreamt them.

And the pattern was always the same, too. He'd turn in a rush, hoping to catch whoever it was that called to him by name. He'd make a complete turn, too, but it was useless. There was never anyone there. No one to see, no one for him to discover. Come to that, he'd also forget the name used by the voice when it called him.

But one thing he did know, was sure of: it was he who was being called. He. No one else.

And one day he broke the pattern; he stopped at mid-circle. He had broken the pattern, and fear had set in, but as it did so—and at that moment—he also realized that it was he who had been calling himself all along. Yes, and this is how (through his own voice), how he found both himself and that pale, fading, childhood year.

This done, he then tried to pinpoint the time he referred to—identified, really—as a *year*.

And, in the midst of all this, he also realized that he thought. That is, that he thought about thinking, about memory, and of time. But further than this, he couldn't go until . . . until his mind would become a blank. No thoughts to be held there, and then, peace, and from peace: sleep. And, it was here, at this point, awake, asleep, and awake again just before dropping off to sleep, that he would hear things, and see them, too . . .

In his sleep, in that wandering year.

Water, Water Everywhere

Texas Winter Garden area heat, remorseless and humid. But a strange heat since it was only the beginning of April. Why, heat like this doesn't come on . . . doesn't settle to wear you down until the end of the month, beginning-a May, or later. But the heat had come on so that the owner . . . the planter . . . couldn't keep up the water supply.

It was hot, and he knew it, too. But where was he then? He'd made two trips that morning, and that was it. And it wasn't enough, not nearly enough, let me tell you that.

The field hands—what else could they do?—they took to going over to a water tank; it was meant for the stock, see? And that's what the planter meant it for, too. He'd said that. So, when the hands went there (you got to understand that it was hot, see?), he'd get angry. Yeah.

Get away from there!

We were getting paid by the hour, all of us was. No piece work, nossir. And he looked at those water trips we took as a waste-a time. And money. But it was hot out in those field rows. What did he know?

Know what he did then? Threatened to fire us, he did.

No more water drinking, hear? Get away from that tank!

But it was the little kids, see? They couldn't do the work, and him not bringing enough water for us. Only made those two trips in the morning, see? So, the kids'd go out to the stock tank.

"Thirsty, Pa . . . That old guy coming over any time soon?"

"Yeah, that's what he said. You hurtin'? For water?"

9

"Mmmmm. M'throat's full-a dust, Pa. Think he'll be here soon? You think I ought-a go to that tank there?"

"Better not. Can you wait a bit? 'Member what he said? About firing us?"

"I know what he said, but . . . It's just that I'm . . . I wish I didn't have to wait."

"That's a good boy. You'll be all right in a while, okay? He'll be here, really."

"Hmmmm. I'll try, Pa. You know, Pa, why ah, why doesn't he just let us bring our own water? We can, you know. And Up North, we always . . ."

"Why? I'll tell you why: 'cause he's no damned good, and he's lazy, and he doesn't care, and that's the way he is."

"We, ah, we can hide the water jugs under the car seat, right? I mean, Up North we can get all the water we want, any time. Right? How, ah, how about if I make like I'm going off the field, to take a leak, see? But near the tank, all the same."

And that was it. Came that afternoon, the field hands'd sneak off—just like the kid said—away from the crops, but near enough the tank.

But the old guy found out right off. He just didn't make out like he had, is all. He was waiting for his chance, see? A chance to grab a whole bunch together, and that way, why, he'd find a way to come up with less wages. Thing is, most of the work would-a been done by late afternoon, but he had the leverage: he could always say no one was working as hard as he'd wanted us to.

What really set him off was a kid. The little guy couldn't wait. He was thirsty, see, but that grower, he, ah, he got angry.

Angry at a kid, can you imagine that? Angry at a kid?

Well, he was going to teach that boy a lesson, he was.

Hmph. What he did and what he said he planned to do were two different things, let me tell you that. Fired off a shot is what he did. To scare him off, he said. Can you beat that? A kid . . .

Shot that boy right in the head. Dead's dead, and he dropped him on the spot. Blood all over the place, the kid's shirt, pants, in the tank water.

Didn't mean to, he said. Hmph. That *didn't mean to* won't bring the boy back, I'll tell you that.

"Well now, I hear that old boy almost went crazy."

"Almost."

"Yeah, he did, and he lost part-a the land, too; and then he took to drinking quite a bit. You know there was a trial . . . or hearing, right? Got off okay, but then he tried to kill himself, he did. Yeah. He, ah, jumped off a tree."

"That kill him?"

"No . . . but he tried to."

"Ah-hah."

"But, look, Compadre, I hear he's gone nearly crazy over this. You seen him lately? Did-ja see the way he was dressed?"

"Look: he dresses that way 'cause he's run out-a cash, that's all."

"Yeah, but still, Compadre . . . you know what I mean?"

"Hmph."

Burnt Offerings

In all, there were five Garcías: Don Efraín and his wife, Doña Chona, and their five-, six- and seven-year-old kids: María, Juan, and the oldest, Raulito. They'd just returned from the Sunday night picture show—about a prizefighter—and it'd been a lot of fun for everybody.

Don Efraín had liked the show so much that he was barely inside the chicken coop when he made straight for the old boxing gloves and then went ahead and put them on the two boys. First he stripped them down to their shorts, then he rubbed alcohol on them—he'd seen the trainers do this—and then he had the two kids to go at it. Doña Chona she tried to stop this on the spot; she knew exactly what the outcome would be: one or both of the kids would wind up mad, crying, hurt and whatnot.

"Look, Efra, why in the world would you want them hitting each other? It just isn't worth it; Juan's going to end up with a bloody nose—he always does, you know—and you also know how hard it is to stop it. And besides that, it's been a long day for everyone and they should all be in bed by now."

"Man, Chona, you ought-a . . ."

"And don't *man* me, Efraín."

"They're playing, that's all. And look, maybe they'll learn how to defend themselves."

"We're not home now, remember? This is a chicken coop. We can hardly move around here, the five of us. And there *you* go making 'em run around, as if we had all the room in the world here."

"Oh, yeah? Well what do you think they do when you

and I are out working in the fields? I just wish they were a little older and that way we'd be able to take 'em to the fields with us. And if we could do that, then maybe they'd help us out, or we could keep an eye on them."

"Oh, sure. You really think so, do you? Look, the older they get, the rowdier they're gonna get. It's part of growing up, Efra. What *I* don't like is having to leave them here, alone."

"You know, wouldn't it be something if one of the kids was real good at this? Boxing. We'd be in clover, Chona. You know jut how much money some of those champs make? Thousands. Yeah, thousands. And this gives me an idea: I'm going to order a punching bag from the catalogue house next week, just as soon as we get paid."

"Well, it's worth a try . . . you never know, you know."

"Right. That's what I've been saying all along."

One of the grower's standing orders was: no children allowed. They'd get in some mischief or other, he'd say. Or they'd take time from their folks, if they had to tend to them. So this meant the nonworking kids had to stay home, in the coops. They'd brought the kids out and kept them in the car once, but the weather had turned brutally hot and humid and they'd all taken sick. So that took care of that. And now the kids stayed home, but this sure didn't take away the worry.

And then Don Efraín and Doña Chona came up with a partial solution: instead of packing a lunch, Don Efraín and Doña Chona would come home at noon. Eat with the kids. Be with them a while.

Came Monday morning, and after a while with each other, off to work. The kids slept on, but this wasn't anything new.

"Efra . . . Efra, you really look happy this morning."

"Ho! And you're the reason, right?"

"Oh, I don't mean *that*. It's more than *that*. What is it?"

"I guess it's the kids, Chona. I love them, and I love you, and I know you feel the same way I do. And I was thinking about how they play with you and me, how they like to play with us."

Around ten or so, the two of them looked up in time to see some smoke. Heavy, dark smoke. From the settlement, no doubt about that now. And then: the chicken coops. Don Efraín and Doña Chona dropped their hoes, ran to the car, and then the rest of the fieldhands did the same and followed them out there, fast, out where they lived. But when they got there, all of them saw it'd been the García chicken coop; and it was going and gone up in smoke.

The seven-year old, that's Raulito, he was the sole survivor.

"The word is that the seven-year old made the other two put the gloves on. They were fooling around—y'know how that goes. But then the boy went ahead and rubbed alcohol on 'em, on María and Juan. And he probably rubbed other junk on 'em, too, for all I know. Just like in the movie, see? But they were playing, that's all. Fooling around, see?"

"Yeah, but how could they just burn up, like that?"

"Well, what happened was that the oldest—Raulito—he started to fry himself some eggs at the same time the other two were goin' at it, and I think something must've happened, and then the little guys burned up; caught fire, see?"

"Maybe he put on too much alcohol on them, you think

14

that's it?"

"Who's to know? Those coops we live in are so damned small, and you know how much stuff we have to keep in there. I don't know, but it could've been the kerosene tank atop the stove. Exploded or something; maybe that's what set them on fire, and the coop, too."

"Yeah, it could've happened that way. Sure."

"And you know what else?"

"What's that?"

"Well, did you notice how the gloves didn't burn up at all? What's the little girl's name? María? Well, she was all burned up, but the gloves sure weren't."

"Well, that's the manufacturers, the people who make 'em. They know what they're doing."

"But what about the Garcías? How're they doing now?"

"They came around; had to. But this ain't something you forget, y'know, and it's going to take time, too. But, I mean, what *can* you do? It's there, waiting for you, but you never know when. Or how . . ."

"God's truth, all right."

Love and Darkness

The lights failed, that's all, went out, but no one knew what could have caused them to go out so fast, just like that, see? And some of the people were really scared; lights off, all over town. No warning, no storm, nothing. And no lightning, either. They were on, and then they were off. Poof! And there'd been a dance on, see?

Now, the people at the dance saw the lights go out first, right away. But some people who'd stayed home, gone to bed early, well, for them it wasn't till morning when they first heard about it. Some a-them must've wondered what was going on, 'cause the lights went out and then the music stopped, flat. But like I said, it wasn't till morning when they found out what had really happened.

"Ramón, he really liked that girl of his; loved her. A lot. And he was a good buddy of mine, too; we were close. And he's the one who told me about her, see? And he was sort-a secretive, but not with me he wasn't; we were friends, see? And he told me he loved her, and he told me more'n once, too. They'd been going steady for about a year, and they'd gone over to the Kress and got themselves some nice engagement rings from there. But don't think it was all his doing, see? She loved him back. It's just that something happened between them last summer. And then, when they met up again, and it had been four months, see, well, when they met up again . . . look: nobody knows for sure, okay?"

RAMON: "A promise is a promise, and I promise I won't even look at another girl. And we both want to get married, right? Okay, now. We *can* run away, elope, if that's what you want. Or we can wait till school's over. How's that? But you're the only one for me. And like I just said, we can run away, if that's what you want. And I can work, for both of us. I know the folks'll get mad and all, but they'll get over it. Would you run away? Now?"

JUANITA: "I think we better wait. It'd be better, wouldn't it? I mean, we better do it right. Proper. And I'll cross *my* heart: I love you. Trust me. Y'see, m'dad wants me to finish school, that's all. And I can't go against him, you can see that, can't you? And I do love, a lot. There. I trust you, and I sure won't see anyone either, Ramón. A promise."

"Who says it's a mystery? *Everybody* knows . . . ha. Don't you tell *me* nobody knows. Listen to this: I heard she ran around when she was up in Minnesota, during the migrant season. But you want to know what else she was doing. At the same time? Well, running around and all, she was still writing letters to Ramón. Yeah, at the same time. Lying to him, of course; and she kept writing those letters to him just the same.

"But Ramón he found out right quick; some friends of his told him all about it, and all about her, too. And I'll tell you how the friends found out. They were working at the same place where Juanita and her folks were staying. So, as soon as everybody came back home—to Texas—they went up and told Ramón right away. First thing, don't you know. Now, *he* was faithful. She was the *one*, see?

"And it was some guy from San Antonio, yeah. That's who she was running around with up in Minnesota. And he was a bag-full-of-wind, he was. One of those sharp dressers, right? Oh, yeah. Orange leather shoes, and he wore one a-them long, drawn out sport coats, and then he walked around with his shirt collar turned up. Cute. Hmph.

"But she liked that, the fooling around part of it. Bound to. What she should've done, but didn't, was to break off with Ramón first. Right? She could've, if she wanted to. When the picking season was over, Ramón and his folks and all the other crews out there, they got back to Texas before Juanita and her folks and their group.

"Ramón, he started getting drunk just about every night. I ran into him a couple of times, you know. And we got to talking. A sliver is what he called it. A splinter or something like that. It's in my heart, he said. That's what women leave there, that's all the're good for. Hurting a guy; taking his heart. Giving it back, full of splinters . . ."

RAMON in Iowa: "Well, I'm through waiting. Soon's I get back to Texas, I'm not putting up with this anymore. We'll just do it, get married. And she'll come, she'll run away with me.

"Every time I pick up this hoe and plunk it down, I can hear her name. Over and over. And why does one feel this way? When one's in love? And then, after work and supper, I sit and stare at her picture till nighttime, but something strange happens . . . The more I look at her—at the picture—the less I remember what she really looks like. I mean, it's her picture all right, but it doesn't look like her. I mean, it's her, but it's not her. At the same time. Yeah, that's it. She doesn't look like the picture, or maybe the other way 'round, the picture doesn't look like her. And the guys rag me about it all the time, but that's okay: I usually go off into the woods anyway to look at the picture. But it's the same thing there: I look at the picture, I stare at it, and then I forget what she looks like. I don't know; maybe I shouldn't look at it so much.

"Faith and trust, she said. And I believe her. Her eyes, that smile; it's the truth, I can remember them all right.

"But I'll be home soon; Texas. And every morning, dawn comes, those old roosters get the day up, and it's just one more day closer to home. And I can see her there, on the streets of home. Pretty soon now."

JUANITA to a friend: "It isn't as if I'm not in love with Ramón anymore. It isn't the same thing at all. I still love him, it's just that I happen to like the way this new guy carries on, that's all. But I don't mean nothing by it, it's just that I like the way he talks. But that's all, okay?

"And then, have you noticed how the other girls stare at him too? Sure they do. And he dresses nice. And what do you mean I don't love Ramón? Of course I do. Where do you get off? I do. All I said was that this guy's nice to me. That's all. He's a nice guy with a nice smile, and he's here . . . Why should I break up with Ramón?

"And what's so bad about my talking with this guy? We talk, that's all. It's nothing serious, see? Besides, I promised Ramón. And that's it. The new guy? Oh, he follows me around; but that's all. It's not that I'm the one doing the chasing. And break up with Ramón? Why? Why should I? I'm not going out with this guy. Like I said, I talk to him, and how about the other girls? You know how they feel? They're jealous, that's all. And that's why I talk to him. But it's Ramón I love, and I happen to love him very much. Look, Ramón and I are going to be together in a few weeks; we'll all be going home soon . . .

"What did you say? What do you mean this new guy is seeing Petra? Is he? Yeah? Well why does he keep tagging after me, then? And not only that, I also get notes from him. Sure. He gets Don José's little boy to give 'em to me."

A note from Ramiro, the new guy:

"I know you're going with somebody else now, but what's that to me? I like talking to you, being with you. Let's meet at Saturday's dance, the two of us. Love you, Ramiro."

"Well, she started dancing with Ramiro that Saturday, and he's the only one she danced with, too. And know what? All her girl friends told her it was wrong, pointed it out to her, but do you think she *cared*? And you know what else? When the last dance came on, they made a date to see each other at home; yeah, Texas. It's hard to see how she could have been thinking of Ramón then and there like she was saying she was. But Ramón, see, he'd already got the word by then. Had to know. The first time she and Ramón met again, and this was after four months, right?, well, he walked up to her, told her off, to her face. Well . . . no. Not at first. I was with him then, and he was happy to see her and what anger he might have had just melted away. But then the more they talked, see? Something happened, all of a sudden, and this really set him off, and so he was angry all over again. And then they broke right there, on the spot; yeah."

The argument:

JUANITA: "You sure you know what you're doing?"

RAMON: "Of course I do."

JUANITA: "And you want to break it off; our understanding?"

RAMON: "That's right. And you want to know something? You dance with somebody else—anybody else—and

20

you're going to be sorry. So don't you do it."

JUANITA: "Says who? You just said we're not going together anymore. We're through, you said. And besides, you haven't got any say-so on who I dance or don't dance with."

RAMON: "Look, whether or not we broke up doesn't mean a thing to me. You got that? I'm getting even. Period. And listen to this: from now, on you're going to do what I tell you to do, and for as long as I tell you. You got that? Nobody makes a fool out of me. You hang on to that. So I'm going to make you pay for everything you've done to me, and I'm going to do it one way or another. It doesn't matter which way, either."

JUANITA: "You stop that. You got no hold on me."

RAMON: "I'm telling you, Juanita. You do what I say, and if you get up on that dance floor, you dance with me or you're not dancing with anyone else, and that's final. You got that, too?"

"But listen to this, though. I heard Juanita had asked her folks for permission to go to the dance, but she asked to go earlier than usual. And she and her girlfriends got there before the band showed up, before they started warming up. And you know why? Hmph: So she and her friends could all stand by the main door. In that way, the guys coming in would see them first. Talk to them; and pick 'em out when the dance started; get it?

"Well, Juanita'd been dancing with just one guy by the time Ramón showed up. First thing he did was to go start looking for her. He found her a-course, but when he did, the dance tune was about over when he walked over to cut in."

"No, I don't know who her partner was or anything; some guy, okay? At any rate, the music starts up again, but Juanita says no; she won't dance with him, Ramón. And I mean they were right in the middle of the dance floor, too. And they stood there, the music playing, the dance going on, people dancing all around them, and there they stood.

"And then they had some words. Know what she did then? She slapped him! Yeah. And then he called *her* a name, and after that, he stomped out, walked on out. With this, she made for one of the benches lining the sides and sat down, just like that. Well, that same dance tune was still playing when all-of-a-sudden-and-just-like-that, the lights went out. Well, people tried to turn them, on, but how? Right? And everyone milled around in the dark, a lot of loud talk, nervous laughter, you know. But no lights came on, no sir. And then someone said the lights had gone out all over town, and that was it for the dance.

"The next day it was, some employees working for the city's utility plant found Ramón; he was dead. The power plant was just a block away from the dance floor. Yeah, they found him, all right: stuck to one of the transformers his hand was. Burned to a crisp, they say. Him, all over. And that's why the lights went out, see?

"But like I said, the people at the dance knew the lights had gone out, but that's all they knew. And you know what else? Some of the people standing by Juanita and Ramón— during the argument—well, they said he told her he was going to kill himself. Can you beat that?

"The folks at home had no idea what was going on. All they knew was that the lights went out. But they didn't find out what happened to Ramón until later; after mass I think it was.

"But it's really a case of love, don't you understand? I mean, those two really and truly loved each other, y'know."

"Well, yeah, if you say so. Hard to tell, though."

With Storms of Prayer

My dear God, and most holy Jesus, it's me again—my third Sunday here, and I come with the same request again—please: Won't you please tell me where my son is? I haven't heard from him—is he hurt? Don't let him, please don't. Save and keep him for me—tell me he's all right, please. I don't want him dead, no, no, not like doña Virginia's boy—he was killed, and he's with You now. But my boy: Save and keep him for me, dear Sweet Jesus, protect him from bullets and wounds and shooting. He's a good boy, yes he is—he's always been a good son and gracious, too. And when I nursed him, a good boy, not once, no, never, not once did he bite or chew or gnaw on me. A good, innocent child. He means no harm—he's good and kind—please keep and save his heart from harm. He's a loving son, yes. Please, please keep and save his heart from harm.

Please, Sweet Mother of God, you tend to him, too. Cover him, and cover his head, and blind the communists, those Koreans and Chinese, please. Protect him from them. Please.

I still have his toys, yes. All his toy cars and trucks, and a kite, yes, I found it the other day, under his old baby clothes. And I've got his school report cards and the comic books he used to read. Everything, see? I've saved everything for him.

Jesus, Son of God, save him, don't let them take him away from me. No: I've made a promise—yes, I have—a promise to the Virgin to visit the Shrines of Our Lady of San Juan de los Lagos in Jalisco, and to Our Lady of Guadalupe, and my boy carries a medal, yes, he made a vow to Our Lady of San Juan down in the Valley. He wants to live: Do take care of him. Take your Hand, take it, and cover his heart—no bullets can enter then . . . he's good and kind, a nice boy.

Oh, he didn't want to go . . . no, he told me so. He was afraid, he said, and yet he was taken away from me. And he cried in my arms, just before he left, and I could feel his heart, and it was like when he was a child and I'd nurse him . . . and then he'd be happy and I was happy, with him.

So care for him, tend to him, cover him. I promise, I promise my life for his. Yes: Bring him back from Korea for me, bring him back safely, unharmed, and do cover his heart, do. God, Sweet Jesus, and Our Lady of Guadalupe, all of You, together, bring him back to me, his mother. Why have you taken him from me? Where is my boy? He's done nothing bad; he's innocent, and he's obedient and humble, yes, he is. He wouldn't harm a soul; not him, no, he wouldn't . . . Please, please: Bring him back to me, alive, alive—I don't want him dead, to die, no.

Look, look: Here's my heart. Go on! Take it! Here, see? Take it—now! Blood? You want blood? Here's mine, if that's what you want. My heart? Is that it? My heart for his? Yes! Now! Here, here's my heart, mine for his, it's the same blood, don't you see?

Yes, that's it; bring him back, bring him back to me, and I'll give you my heart. Please!

Picture of His Father's Face

Nothing to it; all the picture salesmen from San Antonio had to do was to sit and wait, like turkey buzzards, my Pa said, 'cause it was the same every year when the people came back home after some seven months on the migrant trail. There'd be money in their pockets, so, right behind them, the picture salesmen. Nothing to it.

And they brought sample cases of pictures, frames, and black and white and color proofs, too. Here's how they dressed: white shirt first of all, and a tie to go with it. Sure. Respectable, see? And that's why *la raza*, the people, would open their doors to them. I mean, a shirt and a tie represented honesty and respectability. Nothing to it. Easier than stealing, right? . . . and that's what I'm talking about here, see?

You know how people are, how we all of us are wanting our kids to get ahead and be somebody? Wear a white shirt. And a tie. Sure.

And there they came down those dusty streets, sample cases handy, and they were ready to work the town and the people . . .

Once (and I remember it well, too) I'd gone with Pa on a visit; a call to a compadre's house, when one of the sales types shows up. And he looked hesitant at first, kind of timid. Pa's compadre, Don Mateo, he asked the salesman to come on in, sit, make yourself at home.

"Afternoon (he said), you-all doing all right? We got something new to show you this year. Sí, señor."

"Oh, yeah? And what's that?"

"Let me explain what I'm talking about. You give us a

photograph, a picture, right?, and what we do is to amplify it, we make it larger, and that's what amplify means. And then, after that, here's what we do: put that picture on wood. Yes. Sort of rounded off, see? What we call three dimensional."

"And what's the reason for that?"

"Realism. Makes the person come alive, you might say. It-a, it sort of jumps out at you, see? Three dimensional. Here, let me show you this one here . . . This is part of what we do. How about that, eh? Like he's alive, right? It sure looks it, don't it?"

"Yeah, that's pretty good. Hold on a minute, I'm going to show it to my wife . . . (Will you look at this? Isn't that something. Come over here, will you?) . . . You know, we were talking, the wife and me, thinking of sending off some snapshots this year, making them bigger. Enlarging them, right? Ah . . . but this ought to cost quite a bit, am I right?"

"Not as much as you'd think. The problem is *the process*, do you know what I mean by that?"

"Ah-hah. How much money we talking about here?"

"Well, not as much as you'd think, like I said. How does thirty dollars sound? But first-class, rounded off, see? Three dimensional . . .

"Well, thirty dollars does sound kind of steep to me. I thought I heard you say it wouldn't go much more than the old ones. And this is on the installment plan, you say?"

"Well, if it was up to me . . . but it happens that we got us a new sales supervisor this year, and with him, it's cash; cash on the barrelhead, I'm afraid. You know how it is, but he's also right in a way, see? It's good, first class, quality workmanship. It'd make a great picture for that table, see? Realer than real. Rounded off, like this one here. Here, hold it youself. Fine work, right? And we can do it in a month, too. Everything. But what we need from you is to tell us what color clothing, hair, and like that; and then, before you know it, the month's gone by, and you got yourselves the genuine article here. For a lifetime. And listen to this: we'll throw in the frame, too. Free, gratis. And it'll take a month. Tops. And I wish we could do business, but this new supervisor, he wants to get paid on the nail. And he pushes us, see?"

"Oh, I like the work, all right. But it's the money; it's kind-a high."

"I know what you mean. But you got to agree that that's what we call first class goods, substantial, see? . . . and that's what we're looking at here. You never seen work like this in your life, am I right? On wood? Like that?"

"No, I sure haven't, but . . . here, I'll ask the wife again . . . What do you think, eh?"

"It's nice. I like it. A lot. Look, why don't we try one? See how it comes out. We like it, we get some more. Let's start off with Chuy's picture. That's the only one we got of him, though, God rest him . . ."

"She's right. We took it right here before he left for Korea; and he died there. See? Here's the picture we're talking about. You, ah, you think you can do that rounding off with this one? Like you say? Like he looks alive, kind of?"

"Absolutely. We do a lot of servicemen, yes ma'am. You see, in this rounding that we do, they're better than photographs or snapshots. A whole lot. Now, all I need's the size, but you got to tell me that; the size you want. Oh, and that free frame I talked about, you want it in a square shape? Round, maybe? What d'you say? What should I write down here?"

(Don Mateo looked at his wife) "What d'you think? Can we order the one?"

"Well, I already told you what I think. I'd like to have my boy looking like that. Rounded off, in color."

"Okay, write it up like that, but like I said: that's the only picture we got of the boy. So, you got to take good care of it. He was supposed to send us one in uniform, all fitted out, see? And with the Mexican and the United States flags

27

around him. You seen 'em, right? But we never got that picture. What happened was that as soon as he got to Korea, we then heard from the government. Missing in action, they said. Missing. So you best take good care a-that photo there."

"We'll take good care of it, yessir. You can count on it. The company knows you all are making a sacrifice here; oh, yes. We don't want you to worry none. And you just wait when you get it back, cleaned up and everything. What's it gonna be? We put on a navy-blue uniform on 'im?"

"Can you really do that? He's not even wearing a uniform on this one."

"Nothing to it. We just kind of fix it in; what we call an *inlay* job. You know about that? On the wood, see? Here, let me show you these over here . . . See this one here? Well, that boy there didn't have no uniform on when they took his picture. Our company was the one that put it on him. How about that, eh? Blue is it? Navy-blue?"

"Oh yeah, sure."

"And don't you worry none about your boy's picture, okay?"

"How long till we get those pictures, you think?"

"Can't be too long, right? But it takes time on account of *the process*. It's good work. And these people sure know what they're doing, too. You notice? The people in the samples looked alive, real."

"Oh, yeah, I know they do good work, no denying that. It's just that it's been over a month, or more."

"Yeah, but don't forget: how many towns between here and San Antonio? They must've gone through every one, see? It'll probably take 'em more'n a month on account of all the business they did."

"Yeah, that's got to be it, then. Sure."

And then, two weeks after that last exchange, something happened. There'd been some hard rains in the region, and some kids fooling around near the city dump, over by those big drain pipes there, well, that's where the kids found the photographs! Wet, and most beyond recognition, worn out, through and through, and full of holes some of them. But they were the snapshots and the pictures, all right. You could see they were; most of them were the same size, and you could still make out some of the faces on them, too.

Sold! They'd been taken in, and that sure didn't take long to sink in. Taken. Like babies. And Pa's compadre, Don Mateo, he got so mad, so mad, he just took off to San Antonio; went after that guy who'd conned them good, who'd taken their money, who'd taken his Chuy's last picture.

"Well, Compadre, I'll tell you what I did; how I went about it. First off, I stayed with Esteban. Every morning I'd go out with him, to that stall of his, where he sells vegetables; the San Antonio *mercado*, that open-air veg market. Worked with him, loading and unloading, helping out, you know. But I had me a plan, a hunch; a hope, maybe. And I just knew I was going to run across that big city con man, yeah.

"Anyway, every morning after helping Esteban set up that stand of his, I'd walk around some of the barrios there, by the market. Got to see a lot, see? But by now, it wasn't the money so much. That mad kind-of wore off. It was the wife's crying, see? And that'd been Chuy's one and only picture, and we'd told the guy, too. The only one we had of him, and the wife crying all the time. So it wasn't the money so much, now. Oh, we'd found them all there in the sewers, but that snapshot was ruined. Nothing left, see?"

"But in San Antonio, Compadre? How would anyone go about finding a guy like that?"

"I'll make it short, Compadre. He himself showed up at Esteban's stall one day. Just like that! Bought himself some vegetables, he did, right there. And I saw him face to face. He saw me too, but he made out like he didn't know me, know who I was. Never seen me before, see? Oh, I made him right away, and then you know what happened? Let me say this, Compadre, when you're angry, really angry, but I mean really angry now, you don't forget a face or anything. It all comes clear somehow.

"Well, I came up to him, grabbed him, yeah I did, and he went *white* on me, scared. You bet, he was. And I said: 'I want my boy's picture. And I want it rounded off, like you said. Three di—mension. You got that?'

"And then I told him I'd eat him up and spit him out if he didn't come through with that portrait of his. Hmph. He didn't know what to do, where to start. But he did it. From memory, you understand? But he did it."

"Yeah? Well how did he do that, Compadre?"

"Well, that's a mystery, but with fear working overtime, I guess you might say you can remember *anything*, everything. And there it was, three days later, and I didn't have to go after him this time. There he was at Esteban's stall, picture and everything. Well, there it is, see it? Right behind you. Good piece of work, right?"

"Tell you the truth, Compadre, I can't remember what young Chuy looked like anymore . . . But he, ah, he was beginning to look like you, wasn't he?"

"He sure was, Compadre. And you know what people say when they see the picture? They say the same thing. Yeah. That Chuy, had my boy lived, he'd look a lot like me, they say. And there's the picture, here, let me get it for you. I—dentical, eh, Compadre? Him and me, right?"

And All Through the House . . .

Christmas Eve was almost on them, but it was the same old story: the advertising sound truck hired by the Ideal Theater blared out songs of the season mixing, business and heaping blessing on one and all, and now, three days till Christmas Eve, Doña María had made up her mind: *this year* she was going to buy the kids some store-bought toys.

There was always a first time, she'd said, and that decision was firm; final. Nothing new on the promise, however; she'd said the same thing the year before. And the year before that. But it was always the same: no, we can't afford it. And her husband would then bring the same things to the kids: Valley oranges and Texas pecans. But no toys. In that way, her husband would say, and he'd convinced himself by now, they'd each have something; they wouldn't do without.

Nothing new: the kids would ask for *their* toys, her husband would say the same thing: the sixth of January, that's our day. Just hold on till then, okay? The sixth. Epiphany. The Magi. So, every year, Christmas would come, go, the sixth of January would arrive, but by then the kids would either forget or get over their disappointment. But Doña María had noticed something that last Christmas.

About that time, Don Chon, an old family friend, would come over on Christmas night, and he'd bring the sack full of Valley oranges and Texas pecans. Always the same, and Doña María knew it was time for a change . . .

"Why? Why is it that Santa Claus doesn't come to this house, Ma? Why doesn't he bring us something?"

And Doña María: "Of course he comes to see us. Who

do you suppose brings us the oranges and the pecans?"

"Oh, Ma, that's not Santa Claus. That's Don Chon."

"Oh, I'm not talking about that, I'm talking about what's under the sewing machine. What you find there."

"That? That's Pa who puts the fruit there. You think we don't know that? And what's wrong with *us*? Aren't we as good as anybody else?"

"Sure you are! Of *course*, you are . . . All we have to do is wait for the Three Wise Men, and that's when the toys and the presents really come. In Mexico, Santa Claus won't come until the Night of the Magi, the sixth of January. And that's because that's the right *day*."

"Well, maybe, Ma. But what happens is that you and Pa always forget; it goes right by. 'Cause as far as we're concerned, it's been nothing. Nothing on the sixth and nothing on Christmas Eve."

"Well, maybe it'll be different this year."

"Well, yeah . . . maybe. We sure hope so, Ma."

And that's when she decided she'd buy them something. But it was the same old problem for them: they didn't have any cash for the toys. As for her husband, he worked two shifts down at the cafe, worked more than two shifts sometimes, as a cook and dish-washer. And *he* didn't have the time to go Christmas shopping for the kids' toys . . .

And then, what pay they'd have left over at the end of the week, that would go to their savings: the money was needed to pay for their trip to Iowa; the truck driver charged the kids a full fare and even a full fare meant having to stand up from Texas all the way to the Midwest. So, it was him, his wife, and the three boys; that came to a lot of money. But Doña María had made up her mind, and she was going to talk with her husband, that very night, just as soon as he came in from work. She hated to do it since he was so tired, but she had to; she'd made up her mind.

"You know, the boys would like a little something for Christmas."

"Why? What's wrong with the oranges, the pecans?"

"Nothing, really. It's just that they want some toys now. It isn't food they want. They're bigger now, see? They know more."

"They don't need toys."

"Ah, didn't you have toys when you were a kid yourself?"

"It was different then. I made 'em myself: toy soldiers and toy horses. Out of clay, but you know that."

"Of course I do, but it's not the same here; here, they see things and they want them. What d'you say? Why don't we look? Let's buy them something, for once. I'll go to the Kress, myself, really."

"You would?"

"I really would." Resolute.

"I thought you were afraid of going downtown? Remember when we were Up North? In Wilmar, Minnesota? Remember how you got lost there? You sure you'll be okay? You're not afraid or anything?"

"Oh, I remember when I got lost, confused; sure. But I'm okay now; I've been preparing myself all day for this, you'll see. And I won't get lost; listen to this: I go out on the street, right? From there, I can make out the ice house. And that's a matter of four blocks; that's what Doña Regina says. All right: then, when I get to the ice house, I take another right and downtown's right there, two blocks from the ice house, and then there's Kress. After that, from the Kress to the ice house, turn to this street here, and I'm home. How's that?"

"Sounds good to me. I'll go ahead and leave some money on top of the table on my way to work tomorrow morning. But do try to be careful, will you? It's Christmas time, and the streets and stores are both jammed and crowded, and noisy . . . Okay?"

The thing was that Doña María was housebound, and had been for years. The few times she'd venture out it would be to the cemetery, but never alone, or she'd visit her sister and their father a block away, or her own backyard, *el solar*. As for church, she'd go there to the occasional wedding, funeral, but always with her husband and seldom looked to where she was going.

To add to this, her husband had always bought the groceries and what clothes were needed. And so, although downtown was but six blocks away, she'd never been, at all.

She'd seen it, from the back of a truck, as she rode by on her way Up North or back from another migrant season, and once in a while, on a family trip to San Antonio; but other than that, no. As for the long trips, these were normally made late at night; less traffic that way, everybody said.

But this time; this time she meant to walk there alone. She was ready. And so, she arose early, as she always did, served breakfast, as she always did, and she saw to the kids, too; the money was on the table. She started planning her big trip then and there; a smallish shopping district, six blocks away . . . It didn't take her long to get ready.

"I really have no idea why I'm such a scaredy cat; I really don't. My God! Downtown's only six blocks away, and all I have to do is go straight ahead and take a right at the railroad tracks. Then, it's two more blocks and that's it: Kress is right there. To come back from there, it's the two blocks back, take a turn to the left, and that'll put me on this street, and home! I just hope to God I don't meet up with some dog or something else. Or something worse, like when I have to cross the railroad tracks, and maybe some train'll be coming along about the time I have to cross over . . . I hope to God I won't run into no dogs, and no trains, either."

No incident from her house to the railroad tracks, and she'd taken to walking in the middle of the street, too. On the yellow line. No sidewalks for me, she'd said. Some dog could come darting out and then?

Worse: someone might just reach out and grab her. The fact was there was but one dog on the way, but it wasn't there that day. And as far as people are concerned, who'd notice her?

But she hewed to the yellow line, and lucky for her no cars appeared on her way to the ice house. In any case, had there been a car, she wouldn't have known what to do, anyway.

She was now coming up to those railroads tracks and she began to lose her nerve; she could hear the train's engine, the whistle, the deafening noise, and her agitation increased. And now, she couldn't bring herself to cross the tracks; she just couldn't. She'd grit her teeth and head straight for them, head bent low, but she'd come to a dead stop when the train's whistle, blocks away, would blow now and again.

But in the end, she was game. Made up her mind (and closed her eyes) and she made it across the trucks. Courage took over again, and she made the turn to the right; on her way again.

The crowded sidewalks frightened her, but she couldn't walk on the street, not downtown she couldn't. And the noise: dull, incessant, grating. Too, she didn't know or recognize a soul either walking toward her or alongside. And she'd just about decided to give it up, return to the safety of home, but she was bumped ahead by the crowd, and this kept her going toward the center of town.

The noise continued unabated and Doña María heard more than actually saw the people milling about, window shopping, laughing. Fear set in again and a question came to her: Why had she come here? Downtown? With all these *people*? She glanced at a gap between two department stores and dashed in for a breather. It was quieter here; she stared hard at the people walking by and was now steeling herself to go out there, among the crowd.

"Oh, my God, what in the world is the matter with me? It's . . . it's like Wilmar, Minnesota. All over again. I hope to God I won't get sick here; that everything'll turn out all right.

"Let's see: the ice house lies that way. No! The other way . . . Oh, Dear God, what's *wrong* with me? Now, now . . . All right: I was walking from that way there, and then I got here . . . so that means the ice house is over *there*. No, no, no! Good God, I should've stayed home. What am I doing here, *here*?

"Excuse me. Pardon me. ¿Dónde está el Kress, por favor? Ah, Gracias."

She headed where she was told and walked into the Five and Dime . . . But that crowd! And the noise! It was worse here, inside the store.

And now fear bordering on terror, hysteria. What she wanted needed to do, was to leave, get out, away from this place, from these people, the noise . . . But, but, where was the door? All she could see were shapes and things. And people. Things piled atop of things, and people piled atop of people, crushing each other, pushing, shoving . . .

And the objects talked to her, she felt. And then she stopped; stood there, eyes vacant, staring but unseeing. Some of the shapes—the people!—were beginning to stare at her, too. Others merely pushed her out of their way, but she stood firm, remaining in place, dull-eyed, unfocusing. Blinking and focusing now, she made for the toy sections, and she walked to that counter.

She opened her grocery bag and began stuffing it with toys; a billfold? She took that and put it in the bag as well. At this point the noise stopped: she could see the crowds now, and she could see herself walking, her legs moving, and her arms and mouth moving as well. But the noise had stopped. Yes. And then she stopped, turned around, and asked someone for the door, for the exit sign. Someone pointed to it, and she headed that way, but now she was pushing, shoving the people out of her way. When she got to the door, she pushed that, too, and now she was outside, out of that store, away from the noise, and away from the people . . .

She stood on the sidewalk for a moment, trying to get her bearings again when suddenly a hand reached out and grabbed her by the arm, forcibly. The suddenness and the strength of the grasp shocked her.

"Here she is . . . these damn people, always stealing something, stealing. I've been watching you all along. Let's have that bag."

"Bu . . . . . .?"

And now she couldn't hear a thing again, and the next moment the cement sidewalk came rushing at her; a bit of a pebble lodged in her eye, and the pain was awful.

Her arms were grabbed here and there and now she was flat on her back. People looked down on her; they looked misshapen, elongated somehow. And now she could see herself lying on the sidewalk. She *thought* she was talking to someone, but what did those words mean? And yet, there she was: flat on her back and she could see herself, and her mouth, it was moving, talking to someone. A man appeared. Who was she talking to? A man and a holstered gun. Bending over her. I'm out of my mind, she thought.

The kids; the kids! The tears came and she began to cry again. And this was the last thing she remembered.

A sea of people, she could see this; I'm walking through a sea of people; their arms, like waves.

"Lucky for us our Compadre was at the store; he's the one who came running over to the cafe; he told me all about it. How do you feel now? A little better?"

"No . . . I think I've gone mad . . ."

"Well, I was afraid you'd get sick or something, like back in Wilmar, Minnesota."

"Oh, yes . . . and the kids, how're the kids? What's going to happen to them now? What're they going to do now? What's going to happen to them now? What're they going to do with a madwoman on their hands? A woman who can't talk, who can't even go downtown, who . . ."

"So the first thing I did was to get the Notary Public, see? And then he and I ran over here, to the jailhouse. He's the one who talked to the desk man. Told him how you got confused, nervous. That you got scared, outside the house, that crowds made you nervous, right?"

"And what if I'm to be put away? In some madhouse? And then? I don't want to leave the kids, our kids . . . promise me—whatever you do—promise me you won't let them send me away. *Promise* they won't take me away. Ohhhhhh, I should have stayed home! What was I doing downtown, anyway?"

"But you're home now. You're safe here, and you don't

have to go out if you don't want to. And if you do go out, why, stay close to home, in the patio, in the backyard. There's no need for you to go out. Look: it'll be like always; I'll bring everything we need, like I always do.

"And go ahead and cry, okay? It's all right . . . probably the best thing for you right now. And listen: I'll talk to the kids; I don't want them pestering you, fretting you, about no Santa Claus ever again. I'll go ahead and tell 'em the truth: 'Look, kids, there's no such thing as Santa Claus, and that's the end of that.' "

"Oh, no, don't do that! Tell 'em about the sixth; tell them that if Santa doesn't bring them something for Christmas, that he'll make it up to them on the sixth, that the Magi'll bring them something, anything."

"Are you sure? That's what you want, is it?" . . . . . . Well, I guess you're right; maybe in the long run that's the best thing; give them some kind of hope."

The kids, huddled and hiding behind a door, heard their mom and dad. They heard them clearly enough, even if they weren't sure they understood.

And so, it was back to waiting for the Three Wise Men, just like before. January sixth came, but no presents came with it. By now, the kids didn't bother to ask for any, either.

It happened almost immediately. She first went rigid for a moment, just-like-that, and then she was in a trance. Everyone there looked at her closely, intently. They then checked to see if anyone had crossed his legs, arms, hands, anything; to see if there was anything that even looked like a cross. Another look around by everyone, and once satisfied, all were assured that the all-seeing spirit was now in her.

"Who . . . Who among you needs help tonight, brothers and sisters?"

"I'm first. It's about my boy—he's in the service—and I haven't heard from him for about two months now. And then, just yesterday, I got a notice from the Government . . . what does that mean? They say he's missing . . . been missing . . . in action. But what I want to know is: is my boy alive? Is he? I'm going half crazy over this."

"But Julianito is doing well, sister. Yes, he is. Don't worry now—and there's no need to—he'll be home soon, next month. Yes, next month; he'll be here then . . . yours to hold again."

"Thank you . . . oh, thank you so much."

What his mother never knew—she used to set a glass of water under his bed; for the spirits, she'd say—but like I said, what his mother never knew was that it was he who drank the water. Every night. She'd go ahead and place that waterglass under his bed—part of her duty, she said—but he'd drink it right down. She thought it was the spirits, of course, and he never did tell her. He planned to, as soon as he grew up, but he just never got around to it.

The boy needed a haircut, bad; and since the movie house wouldn't open up for another hour, he crossed the street, walked into that barbershop and sat down. And when he did, one a-the barbers, he said something to him. The barber he came up to him again and said he wasn't going to cut his hair.

The kid looked up and thought that the barber meant it'd be a long wait. With this, he then waits for the other barber. And then, as soon as that chair was empty, up he climbs, waits for his turn, but this second barber, he says the same thing: Can't cut your hair. And then the barber went on to say that the best thing for him was to leave the shop. Once and for all; just like that. So, he went back across the street, looked at the movie billboards a while, but here comes that first barber. And he told him to go away, to get away from there.

It was then—finally—that the kid got the message, and he headed for home. To get Pa, he said.

"Hey! Why do you guys go to school so much for, anyway? What's the use?"

"My old man, my dad, he says we got to be ready. 'Cause someday there just might be an opportunity, a chance, see, and we may be the ones to get it."

"What are you talking about? Look, if I was you, that'd be the last thing I'd worry about. Let me tell you something: we're in a hole—all of us, see?—and we ain't getting out of it. Got that? There's just no getting out-a that hole . . . so why worry about it? Now, you know who's got to hump it? *They* do; the ones on top . . . they got more to lose, they got to be careful they don't fall in the hole with us. You understand? You see, if they're not on their toes, they're going to wind up down here, with us. But as for us? Shoot! We're about as low as we can get. Yeah."

That schoolteacher didn't know what to do, what to think, what to say . . . Here they all were, by the classroom bulletin board, when all of a sudden, this Mexican kid pops a button from his shirt and hands it to her. Here. Take it.

Sure, the class needed something to set off the town's button factory, but . . . And it was probably his only shirt, too. Had to be.

Questions. But who's to answer whywhywhy? Did he, did he mean to help? Be part of the group? Did he do it for *her*?

Why?

He did it because he had to, he wanted to. She felt this. A desire, that's what it must have been. An overwhelming urge, the intensity of it all. She sensed this. Felt it. The intense feeling of wanting to give, of giving.

But she couldn't explain it; not to anyone; not to herself.

Migrating time again, and just before *la raza*—the people—headed Up North, the priest'd come over and start blessing the cars and trucks: five bucks a shot. And one time, he made out pretty good . . . good enough to go to Barcelona—that's in Spain to see his folks.

Well—as a token of thanks, I guess—he brought back some picture postcards; one a-them showed this big old church. A cathedral, *he* called it. And then the priest, he tacked up those postcards at the front, right where you come in. People'd admire the cards, look hard at that *cath*-edral, see; and then—just maybe—then they'd get to working for one just like it, is what he thought.

Well, sir, wasn't long before someone or somebody takes to writing on them cards he put up. Started marking them, too, with crosses and everything, a line here, another there and writing *con safos*—with a *s*, yeah—*con safos*, ha! Better you than me, right?

The priest, he just couldn't understand it; called it a sin and a shame, a *sacrilege*, yeah, that's what he called it.

Oh, and it was such a lovely day for a wedding! All week long, the groom-to-be (and his father, too) worked on his future wife's backlawn—mowing, cutting back, setting up the truck tarp for the reception line, and like that. That backyard was all worked over; decked out in Texas Pecan branches, Indian paint brush, wild lilies, hollyhock; and then—careful, now—the tamping down all around the tarp; smooth as glass it was.

And water. They watered the dancing area first of all, and then they watered it down some more. There. Hard; smooth, there, that'll hold the dust in time for the dance.

After the wedding ceremony, the couple walked the length of main street toward home amid cheers and laughter. The groomsmen and bridesmaids trailed right behind them, but up front: the neighborhood kids: yelling, and whooping and hollering—Here they come, everybody! Here come the bride and groom!

Yes, a beautiful day; just a great day for a wedding.

"Comadre, what's this I hear about you-all going to Utah?"

"No, Compadre, where'd you hear that? Besides, we just don't believe that new labor contractor . . . He says he's taking people to, to . . . what's the name a-that place, again?"

"They call it Utah, Comadre. But what is it . . . you don't trust the contractor?"

"Well, what if he's just making up the name a-that state? Have you ever heard a-that Utah, Compadre?"

"Well, no, but there's a lot of states out there, you know; and, well, it's just that this is the first time they're hiring people to go there, and that's why it sounds strange."

"Yeah, sure . . . but . . . all right, tell me this: You yourself ever heard a-that place?"

"No . . . not really; not having been there before, see? But I hear tell it's by Japan, or close to it."

Here was a chance to quit working in the fields as stoop labor . . . One of those Protestant preachermen from town had driven over to the migrant farm shacks: A man was coming, the preacher said. A man who was going to teach them the trades: carpentry, and such. This'd get them out of the hot sun.

Most of the grownups thought it a fine idea . . . an opportunity.

About two weeks later, a man showed up, just like the preacher said he would. Came in driving a pickup and the pickup, it had a trailer house in the back.

The preacher's wife showed up, too; she was going to help; pitch in as a translator.

So, what happened? Well, those two they went into that air conditioned trailer house and stayed there that whole day. Stayed there the week, inside that trailer house, and then one day they pulled out. Took off.

Word was that the woman had left her preacher-husband for the carpenter or whatever he was . . .

It was just a few minutes before six, about the time the spinach cutters usually come in from the fields. The first thing we heard right off was the siren atop the water tower; this was followed by the siren on the firetrucks, and then the ambulance, last of all. Some of the other fieldhands filled us in:

That one of the trucks, one loaded with-a bunch of people, had been in a wreck. With a car, they said. That the truck was on fire, and burning real hot. One-a them new pickups— a van, they call it—all sealed up, and only a few made it out in time.

The witnesses—'cause they saw it—they said that that van just about blew up then and there and burned everybody in it; it-just-caught-fire, they said. And a-those who jumped out in time, well, some a-them was on fire themselves, hair and everything.

The Anglo woman—she was driving the car—well . . . she was drunkdrivin'.

They say she lives in one a-them dry counties around here, but the reason she got drunk was on account a-her husband: ran out on her, they say. Yeah.

How many dead? About sixteen, I think; that's what I hear.

"I hear Figueroa's out on parole; is that right?"

"Yeah, but he's a sick man. I hear tell that up to Huntsville—that state prison there—they'll give you shots; vaccinations, if they take a disliking to you. Them things are meant to do you in."

"Nah . . . where'd you hear stuff like that, anyway? . . . Any idea who turned him in?"

"Some Anglo guy, more'n likely. Way I figure it, he must-a seen Figueroa walking downtown with that little blond thing; the one Figueroa brought down from Wisconsin . . . And where was Figueroa gonna get himself an attorney, eh? And then, to pile bad on top-a worse, they say that little old blond thing was underage. Seventeen, and that's against the law."

"Tell you what: five bucks says he won't last a year here."

"I dunno as I'll take that bet. He's got something in him. A rare disease, they call it."

Bartolo, he was the town poet, and he'd show up about the time he figured the people'd be coming back home . . . home from Up North after all the work, around December. And he'd localize the poems, and this'd then give the people a chance to see their names in print; yeah.

And he usually would sell out everything on that first day back. Just about.

Oh, and then he'd read the poems. He'd read 'em serious like. Emotional, and solemn, too. And this is true, too: I remember he told the people—*la raza*—to read his poems aloud . . . where they could *hear* them, he said. And then he'd say this: the human voice seeds love in the dark, or, the voice is love's own seed in the dark. Something like that; real pretty.

The old man—his grandfather—was felled by a stroke; left him paralyzed. He spent his days sitting on a big oak chair, thinking. And then one day, a grandson of his came in for a visit . . . to *platicar*, he said; chat a bit.

That old man asked the boy how old he was, and what was it—above all else, now—what was it he wanted the most, if he could have it. The youngster said he was twenty. Twenty-years old, but what he wanted—really wanted, and most of all—was for time to go by, in a flash. And in this way, he said, he would then know what his life would be like, ten years from now.

The old man looked at him and then looked far, far away.

"Why, that's the stupidest thing I heard yet." He said that, the old man, and then he didn't say another word; wouldn't even look at the boy.

The grandson was stunned . . . stung, too, I'll bet. What does he mean *stupid*?

Took him ten years, but when he hit thirty, some of the answers started coming to him.

And When We Get There

On the road, four in the morning, and that's when the truck broke down. The sudden stop brought a halt to the whining of tires on pavement and this roused some of the fieldhands. Most were still stupified, hypnotized almost, by the steady whine and woke up with a start when the truck came to a dead stop by the side of the road.

Silence. Something must've happened; the motor had been acting up lately, heating up; that must've been it.

The driver did make one more try to rev it up again, but he did it more out of habit than from anything else.

And this would have to be home for what was left of the night, where this place was, at four in the morning. One had to wait, and then, at daylight, someone would hitch a ride to the nearest town. Wherever that was.

Awake now, a few of the fieldhands—men, women, and youngsters—talked in low tones. Most of them went back to sleep and desultory conversations opened up only to close again. The two sounds, their hushed tones and the chirping of the crickets, mixed in the open air, as the ten-tire truck rested on the shoulder of the two-laned blacktop. There was talk here and there amid the light snoring; others, awake, too, but not talking, looked dully into the night, thinking . . .

". . . good thing it stopped *here*. I had to go; bad. Good thing the truck died when it did. Shoot, I'd have had to wake up half the truck cutting through the people and thumping on the window of the cab to get them to stop.

"It's still kind-a dark, though. Wonder what time it is? It doesn't matter; I'm getting off this thing, and I've got to find me a place to *go*. A ditch somewhere; anything.

"Must have been the picante sauce that did it; it might have gone bad on me. But then I went ahead and ate all of it. Yeah, waste not, want not. . . . But I can't see where I'm walking.

"Hope the wife's okay and her having to hold on to that boy of ours. Can't be helped, though, she's got to hold on to him in this crush. . . ."

"I think we're in luck. We drew us a good driver this season; steady, goes at a good clip, and he won't stop unless absolutely necessary. Take on some gas and there we go again."

"Let's see, we took off yesterday morning about this time. Yeah, I'd say we've been on the road some twenty-four hours. That means we're closing in on Des Moines."

"But I'm kind-a stiff. Sure wish I could sit down somewhere for a bit. I'd just as soon get off, too, lie down on the road, but . . . you never know what's going to be down there. A snake or something."

"I, ah, I fell asleep standing up, but I woke up a couple of times when I felt my knees giving way. Funny what the body can do, put up with. Sleep a little, wake up, and like that."

"But it's the kids, see? They got to stand up, too. Now, they really get tired, no two ways on that.

"Poor little guys. And they can't even grab a-hold of something, like those two by fours which hold the tarp in place."

"That driver must've loaded forty of us on this trip, but I remember the time we had some wetbacks with us and there was some sixty of us then. Sixty's quite a bit, and I could hardly light a cigarette in that mob."

"You seen a dumber woman in the world? In your entire life? What was she doing? I mean, what was the thinking about? Here this diaper loaded full and *she* throws it *forward*! Damn thing came right back, slid on that tarp, and damn!

"Good thing I had them glasses on, man, otherwise I'd a-got shit in my eyes, know what I'm saying? Dumb? No, there's got to be another word for her."

"Jesus! What in hell was she thinking about . . . it's 'cause and effect, man. Couldn't she see what the hell was going to happen? Shit flying every which way? Jesus! And she could've waited, right? Bound to be some gas stop or something, and then she could leave that shit there. . . ."

"You should've seen that black man. 'I want fifty-four hamburgers, partner.'

"At two in the morning. I walked in that little place, and he couldn't have seen the truck 'cause I walked a good piece before I got to that hamburger joint a-his.

"I said, 'fifty-four hamburgers' and his old eyes bulged out. Two in the morning, fifty-four.

"And he said, 'Man you must eat one hell of a lot.' The thing was that the people hadn't eaten all day and the driver, he said the best thing to do was to save time, to avoid stopping, and that the best thing too was to have one person go get something to eat for everybody.

"That black man, though . . . surprised? You wouldn't believe how surprised he was. 'Fifty-four? Is that right?' "

"You know what I think? I think that at two in the morning, and hungry, I think you could put a good dent into fifty-four a-them Wimpy's. . . ."

"Listen to this, and *listen* to what I'm saying: This is the very last time I'm coming up here. We get to that farmland we're going to this year, and I'm walking. Walking the hell out and heading for Minneapolis. Get me a damn job there. Anything.

"Me back to Texas? Up yours! Say what you want, but you get to earn a living here, Up North. I'll go hunt for that uncle of mine, and he'll get me something. Maybe a job in some hotel or something. Be a bellboy, yeah. Maybe I can come up with something in that hotel; get some kind-a break, see? There or at some other hotel, I don't care."

"And now about those Viking girls? They're going to have to stand in line . . ."

". . . and with that money Mr. Thompson loaned to me, I figure we can make do, eat and live on for something like two months. By then, see, we'll be drawing our pay for the sugar beet season.

"Sure hope we don't get too much in debt, though. Y'see, with these two-hundred he come up with, I had to spend about half on the trip 'cause now I got to pay for the kids, too. Half price, sure, but I still got to pay for them. And when we get back, it's four-hundred I got to pay back. And that's double, right? But what's the choice? So, I got to come up with four-hundred. I know it's a big interest, but when you need the money, you got to get it from somewhere.

"Now, some people've come up and told me to turn him in to the law for him charging too much . . . Well, he's already got the deed to our house, see?

"Sure hope that sugar beet season's a good one, otherwise . . . otherwise, we start eating air, and that's a hell of a diet.

"And we got to come up with that four-hundred. After

that, we'll see how much we can come up with . . . and these little guys, they got to go to school and all. And that'll take a chunk, right?

"But, ah, but it's always chancy with us, isn't it? I mean, we *hope* everything turns out for us, but if it don't, well, if it don't, we're up against it again. And so what's new, right? About the only thing I want from God is a place for us to work in."

"Fucking fucked-up life! That's what it is . . . a crazy, worthless, fucked-up fucking life. And you know why it is we live this way? 'Cause we're assholes, that's why. Every damn one of us: fucking assholes.

"And it's a fucking assholish life, too. But no less than we deserve for being the assholes that we are, right?

"Goddammit to hell, and I'm the one leading the way. But this is it! This is the very last goddam time I'm coming up here like some fucking pack mule, standing every inch, foot, and mile in every state a-the goddam way.

"The last time! Anybody got ears 'round here? You just wait: just as soon as we get there, it's Minneapolis here I come!

"And what do you mean work at what? Hmph, don't you worry about *that*. I'll *make* something, goddammit.

"One a-these days, I'm going to take my pecker out and let the world blow on it. And this life? Well, it's my fault, my own goddam fault 'cause I'm a dumbass, and I'm the one who let 'em *do it* to me, and that's why I'm an asshole!"

". . . I know my husband's tired. Been on his feet since we started out on the trip. Saw him nodding off, I did. I'd help him if I only could, but . . . but I'm carrying these two.

"I wish we were there now; that hardwood floor be soft enough after this. And the babies . . . they'll beat you down, work you to death.

"I just hope I can help him, somehow, out in the fields this year. But with these two? And I have to be with them all the time. And nurse? Every five minutes, it seems like. But they're so little, they just tie you down. Wish they were older.

"Still, I'm going to give it a try. I'm going to try my best to help him out on the hoeing and the chopping . . . but not on the picking, though. I'll follow him, keep him company in the beet rows; that'll help, he won't get so tired then.

"I know what; I'll do it in bits and pieces, a little at a time.

"And he's so funny, they're babies and he's talking about them going off to school already. I hope to God I can help, be of help to him. And I will, God willing."

"And will you look at those stars? From out here they look like they're touching the tarp, coming down to it. And so quiet you'd swear there wasn't a soul in the truck over there. And there's hardly any traffic, not at this hour. A trailer once in a while, but that's about it. And the silence at this hour. A soft silence is what dawn is. Soft as silk.

"One thing'd be nice, though . . . what if it were always like this: a nice, soft dawn; quiet, like silk.

"But I bet we're still here at noon. By the time they get to town, find help in town, and by the time they get around to fixing the engine or whatever . . .

"But if it were always like this, dawn . . . who'd complain then? I'm going to look at the sky, the last star. And I wonder how many people in the world are looking at the same star right now? And how many others are thinking about those who are thinking about keeping an eye on that last star? And it's so quiet, too; quiet enough to imagine, to hear, maybe, that the crickets are talking to the stars."

"This damn truck! Nothing but a damn nuisance, that's what it is. A nuisance and a damned botheration. Yeah. I know what I'm going to do just as soon as we get there. I'm chucking this old heap, yeah, and these damned people can damn well look out for themselves.

"I'll drive them out to those farmlands, leave 'em there like I told 'em I would, and then to hell with it. I'm gone!

"And I didn't make no contract with them. They paid me, I brought them here, and how they're going to make it back to Texas is up to them. And besides, someone'll come by, pick 'em up, take them back to where they came from.

"And I'll say this about that sugar beet crop: the money's just about played out, it ain't the paying proposition it once was. Not like it used to be, not like in other years.

"Best thing for me to do now is to get right back to Texas, yeah, and I will just as soon as I get rid of them back there. And then I'm going to try the watermelon business, I'll truck me some. And it's close to watermelon time now, too.

"Damn! All I need now is not to be able to find someone who can work on this damn thing. And if I don't? What then? And those damned cops better not come 'round here, telling me to move on like they did in that other town; bunch-a shits.

"And who was stopping, goddammit? We was passing through, that's all. But that big-ass cop he caught up with us, and gave me one a-those 'Okay buddy, keep it moving, just follow the highway, and keep your nose straight ahead.'

"Show-off shit, grandstanding for the town folks he was. And who the hell was stopping? Goddammit!

"You just wait; just as soon as we get there, I'll deliver

'em, sort 'em out, and I'm gone! After that, why, it's every man for himself."

"... and when we get there, I'm going to see about a bed, a soft one, for my wife. Her kidneys are giving out on her. A bed, 'cause last year . . . and what if this year's chicken coops have cement floors, just like the ones last year? *Then* what?

"And that floor was *cold*; it didn't matter how much hay we'd spread or pile around it. Nothing. Cold is cold, and that's what the floor was.

"She can't take it, and she shouldn't. And I bet that's why the rheumatism flared up on me last year. Sure as shooting' . . ."

"... just as soon as we get there. Sure. Just as soon as we get there. But here's the plain truth of that. I'm tired of getting there. Gettin' there's just like leaving . . . Yeah. Sure.

"What's the difference? Coming and going, going and coming. Right? And the truth is . . . the truth is I'm tired of *getting there*. Hmph. Probably be better if I said, just as soon as we *don't* get there, 'cause that's closer to the truth: We *never* get there.

"... just as soon as we get there, just as soon as we get there. . . ."

The crickets didn't stop their chirping all at once; they'd chirp here and there and now and again. Maybe getting tired of it themselves. And dawn wasn't holding back either, but it was more subtle than the crickets.

A light here and then one over there; a clump of something became a wild apple tree, for instance. Little by little as if afraid people'd find out what it—dawn—was up to.

A light would then spring up over there and some rounded objects would become people and not dark, slow-moving shapeless things.

And when the light did come, *la gente*, the people, alit from the truck and gathered 'round it and each other. And what did they talk about?

They talked about what people always talk about, about what to do, about what they'd do just as soon as they got there. Someplace.

This Migrant Earth

It was his mother's crying that set him off. And worse, his mother wasn't crying for herself alone, and so, he felt anger. And hatred. Ma was crying for his uncle, and his uncle's wife, Auntie. T.B., the doctors said. T.B.

Each was carted off to a different sanatorium. This meant that the other aunts and uncles took in the kids; family's family, they said. True, it had been hard on everyone, but family's family, and that's what family means.

And then his aunt died, and it wasn't long before his uncle was brought home. Too late, they said; spitting up blood, they said.

And that was the morning he saw his mother—Ma—crying. The anger he felt was real enough, but what could *he* do?

And then? His own Pa! So the anger that had not gone away, renewed itself and then hatred came with it. *This* time, this time it was Pa—*his* Pa.

"Oh, sonny, you, ah, you should've brought him in earlier, sonny. Earlier. He was sick, sonny; you couldn't see this? It's that sun, sonny, it beat him down. Beat him to the ground. You shouldn't . . . and the kids, too."

"I couldn't tell, Ma. I mean, we were all of us sopping wet, sweatin', and you don't feel the heat then, right? But . . . but you're right, Ma. It's different when the sun gets to you, isn't it? I mean, Pa'd been struck, right? Only we didn't see it, didn't know it. Beat by the sun. And it's different in his case, isn't it? I mean, I'd told him to go on in and rest, 'Go to that tree yonder,' I'd said. But he wouldn't. Didn't want to. And when he began to throw up then . . . get sick, like that. And then we saw he couldn't hold on to the hoe, and that's when the other kids 'n me dragged him over to the trees. And he didn't fight us off, either; he really did let us carry him. Didn't say a word or anything."

"That poor suffering man. And you know he didn't sleep at all last night, don't you? Could you hear him last night, when he went outside? He was in pain, bent over he was. Like he had the cramps all over his body. God rest him, I hope he comes around soon; you see, all morning I've been giving him some lemonade, trying to cool him down somehow. You see his eyes, sonny? Watery and glassy, they look. I shouldn't have let him go out to the fields with you-all . . . Nothing would've have happened then; nothing. And he's such a good man, your Pa. And he'll suffer with these cramps for three days and nights, 'cause that's how long those things last. And you-all better watch it, too. And don't you work so hard, you hear? That landowner he tries to hurry you, don't pay him no mind. You understand? He says 'hurry it up,' you-all throw down those hoes, you kids hear me? I mean it, sonny. He finds it easy work, does he? Let him try it; he doesn't have his rump and tail sticking out to the sun all day long. Everyday . . . What does he know? What does he care?"

And this time Ma did mean it, but the boy was still angry, angrier if anything. And even more when he'd hear his dad—his Pa—moaning and groaning out by the chicken coops. Where they slept. His Pa couldn't stay inside the coops, though. He just couldn't. He'd choke, suffocate, he said. Now, outside, he said, outside the air would get to him, and he could breathe. And on the grass. Yes, he could stretch out there. And then when the cramps'd come and him being out on the grass there, that helped some. He could roll there, when the cramps bit into him and doubled him over.

And suddenly this thought came to him: would his dad die? Could his *Pa* die? From the sun? A moan, and the boy turned to his Pa. Pa was praying! Pa, praying to God, wanting God to help him, somehow.

He thought his dad would get better the next day. And when he didn't, the boy became angry. Angrier. And angrier still when his mother—not angry at her, no—but angrier when he'd hear both of them begging for God's help.

Begging God to help *them*? What had *they* ever done to anybody?

His Ma had gotten up then. She removed the scapularies (they were supposed to *help* him) and she washed them. She then lighted some votary candles. Nothing. It was his uncle and aunt, all over again.

Alone:

"Why does Ma waste her time washing that stuff, lighting those candles there; that sure didn't help Unc or Auntie, either. Why does Ma keep *doing* that?

"And how is it *we're* the ones? Like we've been buried alive here, on top of the earth? And when it isn't TB, it's something else. The sun! Always sick, somebody is. Why *is* that?

"And there's my dad . . . no one can say he's a loafer. He works hard. He was born working. There he was, he says, five-years old, barely five-years old, and he was already working out there . . . with *his* Pa, planting corn.

"What's the use? Why? Here we are: feeding this *earth*, feeding *it* and feeding the sun, too. And *then* what? That sun just beats you down, to the ground . . . on your knees.

"And what can *we* do? Nothing. That's what; nothing. And then Ma and Pa pray to God, of all things. God doesn't care. He doesn't even know we're *here*.

"Shoot! I don't think there's such a thing as G . . . Hmph. What if I say it? What if Pa gets worse? *Then* what? I don't know, maybe praying's good for them, if it makes 'em feel better."

His mother could see how angry he was—raging almost. So she tried to get him to calm down; it's in God hands, she'd say. Pa'll be all right, you'll see, with God's help."

With his mother:

"God's help? What? God doesn't care, Ma. He doesn't. Not about us, He doesn't. God's help. All right, all right, tell me this, then: what kind of man is my Pa? A bad man? A good man? Mean-hearted, is he? My Pa? When's he *ever* hurt anyone? Taken advantage of anyone? Well, Ma? Tell me that."

"No, your Pa's a good man, but that's not the point, sonny. No . . ."

"No, Ma. That *is* the point. He's a good person, Pa is . . . And Unc? And Auntie? Dead, both of them. And my cousins? Why, they're going to grow up never having known their parents; yeah. Ha! God doesn't care, not about us, at any rate . . . And not about the poor. No.

"And listen to this, too, Ma: tell me this. You ready? Why is it we have to live this way? Suffer like this? Why us? Who have *we* ever harmed? Ah? And you? You're a good person, Ma. A *good* person."

"No, no, no, sonny. You mustn't talk that way. You mustn't say that. Don't you *ever* talk that way again, not about God, not against God. His word! Please, please, sonny. Please. I'm scared already, and then you go ahead and scare me some more with that kind of talk . . . You . . . I mean, I know that you don't . . . but it's like the Devil's got into you somehow. In your blood, somehow."

"Maybe, Ma. And why not? I'll probably be better off that way; yeah. And then maybe the anger'd go away. But it's got to where I can't think anymore, Ma. Why us, Ma? Why-whywhy? And why *you*? Pa? M'uncle? And my aunt, too, why? Why her? And their kids? Why them? Why should they be made to suffer? Tell me that. *You* tell *me*, okay?

"Why *us*, Ma? Why should we be treated like animals, yeah. Animals . . . without hope. And here's what really kills me, Ma. You know what kind-a hope we got? Do you, Ma? *Our* hope is that *we* make it back here, to this place, next year. That's some hope, that is. And, and, and like you say, we'll rest when we die. But who wants *that*? Rest when we die . . . hmph. But that's what happened to Auntie and Unc, Ma! Does Pa feel that way? Believe that? Does he?"

"Yes. Yes, sonny, that's how it is. Death. Death will give us peace. And rest."

"No! Why us, Ma? Us!"

"You have to believe . . . I mean, it's written that . . ."

"Allrightallrightallrightallright. All right, okay, Ma? I know what you're going to say. I know exactly what you're going to say: 'The Poor Are Going to Heaven.' Right?"

The next morning started off as a cool one; cooler, anyway. And cloudy. A slight cool northern breeze; he felt it skim by, fluttering his eyelashes. He and his two kid brothers started the day's work. Hoe up, hoe down. Chopping weeds.

His mother stayed at the chicken coops. Had to, she was taking care of Pa . . . this meant the boy was in charge of the kids, and he began to urge them to work, hurry them up, like his Pa.

Most of the morning had stayed cool, and cloudy, and the sun had let up somewhat, but it wouldn't stay cool for ever. An hour later, the sun broke through the clouds, swept them away, and the heat of the day settled in to stay, to keep them company, they said.

They worked well enough, but the heat would make them slow down a bit, and because of the heat, they tired faster. But it was the sun that was working against them. So, whenever they tried to hurry, to catch up, to do more work, the heat beat them back. And, it was a clammy, sticky heat; sweat would run into their eyes, and when they rubbed, the sweat crept in their eyes, made them cry and, at the same time, this caused their eyesight to blur. It was the blurring; this was the danger sign. They knew.

To the kids:

"Listen now: you start getting dizzy, blurry-eyed, you slow it down some; take it easy, okay? And, when we get to the edge of the rows, stop. Rest a bit. It was nice this morning for a while, but it's going near to noon now, and it looks like a hot one from now on in. Be different if it was cool, cloudy. But it ain't, okay? So don't hurry none. It's the sun that's scaring all those clouds away. But that ain't the worse of it, compared to what's coming up.

"I figure we'll get through here 'round two or so, and *then* we go to that patch across the way. And that's gonna be the hard part. It's the hills, the rises, see? Up and down, just like the hoe, see? Now, it's okay on the up part, 'cause there's some breeze there; it's the coming down, see? In the gullies down there, there's not a bit-a air, let me tell you. That air just can't make it down there. You hold on to that. Okay?"

"Yeah . . . sure."

Half an hour later:

"All right, since we're gonna catch the hottest part of the day hoeing up and down on the chop by those knolls there, don't forget to drink the water. You drink as much as you can, got that? Every now and then, okay? Don't go too long without it. And listen, it doesn't matter what the grower says if he comes over. If you're thirsty, you stop work and get yourself a drink. And *do* it! Never mind the grower; you get yourself some water.

"I don't want you coming down sick, now. You start feeling bad, you stop right there and do it! You just let me know . . . and as soon as you do, we go straight home. Okay? You remember what happened to Papa? Huh? You saw him, right? He overdid it, see? That sun'll eat you right up . . . it will."

It was just like he said. They'd moved over to the new patch, and it was hot. By three o'clock, they were wetting up again, parts of the sweat coming through the clothing. And they found they had to stop more often now, just as their brother had said. They had trouble breathing, and once in a while, one of them would get blurry-eyed, and he'd stop. A bad sign, just like Pa.

At the other patch, the grower:
"How's it going, guys? Working hard? Kind of hot, eh?"
"Whew. It's just too hot to work sometimes. But we'll go on till six here."

To the older brother:
"We've been drinking water like you said, but it won't cut the kind a-thirst we got. We were talking, Older Brother, sure wish we had some good-old-well water. Fresh. Cool. Yeah. Or maybe a Coke. Yeah, a Coke'd do it . . . real cold . . ."

"What are you kids talking about? You drink something that cold and then you'll really come down with something serious. Yeah, you will. Look. Just slow it down, that's all. The grower knows how hot it is; we just go on till six, like we told him. What d'you say? Six? Can we make it?"

But they didn't make it till six o'clock. Along about four or so, the youngest kid got sick on 'em. And here he was, his youngest brother, barely nine-years old and drawing adult wages. Yeah, he was. And that's why he was pushing himself, trying to do as much as the others, the olders guys. His own kid brother doing that. The first thing he did was to throw up; and then he sat down, for a bit he said. But then he rolled over, flat, out.

The older brother saw this and the youngest standing by him got scared. What's the matter with him? And now the nine-year old had his eyes shut, tight.

So now the older boy had to pry his brother's eyes open, and when he did, all he could see was the white part; at this point, the youngest started to cry.

Here, the boy said, let's get him out of here. C'mon. The two of them began to carry the nine-year old; and the kid, in a dead faint, got the shakes, like he was cramping up on them. The older boy began to carry his kid brother by himself, and as he did so, he started off again: whywhywhy.

"First my dad now him, my kid brother. Why? He's nine-years old! Why? Look at him: a nine-year old boy sweating like he was a work animal! Why? What's my Pa ever done to anyone? In his life? And my Ma? Well? And now him, my kid brother. Why?"

And with every step he took there was that whywhywhy. On their way home now, and he's becoming angrier and angrier still. Halfway home now, and here's when he burst out crying!

But there was anger, resentment, in that cry. And then the other, smaller brother began to cry; out of fear, mostly, but what could *he* do?

And now the boy carrying his brother and caring for all, began to swear. Swear and say things that had been stored up, welled up for a long, long time. And he said them. And they needed to be said, he felt. No time to stop and think *when* he started saying those things. They flat needed to be said, yeah.

So, he swore at God himself. Right at Him. Cursed Him up and down, up and down, like the hoe. And then he became fearful; there had been too many years of training, advice, whatever, from his parents and family. He had to be scared.

But then he looked to the ground. And the anger returned: whywhywhy. This earth, he said. And if it opens up for swearing at God just like Ma said? And if it eats me up for calling God a . . . and he looked down again, for a moment there he was, sure that the earth was ready to swallow him whole. Gobble him up, whole . . . But no. The ground was harder, if anything. Yeah, if anything, it was harder now than ever before. And the stored anger came right back.

After this, he began cursing God again. He then looked at his kid brother—the one he was carrying—he *looked* better, he thought. But was he? And then he thought on what he'd *said*. Did the little kids know, understand what he'd said? He'd yelled out some terrible things, screamed out some horrible things, yes, but did they understand what it meant?

And now they were home, but tired as he was, he wasn't about to go to sleep or rest, just yet. Instead, he stayed up late, alone; and he then found he was at peace, at rest. And that peace was like nothing he'd ever known before. He felt apart, removed from everything around him; isolated like.

But at peace in that isolation. And he was no longer worried about his dad or about his kid brother or about what he'd said, either. He now looked toward the new day, that very next day. The cool morning, its fresh breeze.

He got up at first light and found his dad—his Pa—doing well. Much better, in fact, and getting stronger, too. Coming around. And the kid brother, he too was doing better. A cold shiver, a minor cramp now and again, but doing better, cured almost.

But yesterday lingered on his mind, and what he'd *said*. Himself surprised, awed, too, and shocked at times by what he'd said. He was about to tell his mother but he stopped: no. He decided against telling her almost as soon as he thought about it. He was also about to tell her that the earth didn't open up, didn't swallow people whole. She'd said this to him sometime back, and she believed it. But he didn't. She believed that the earth would open up and eat those who cursed God. But not me, he said. No.

Well? He'd done it, and here he was on top of the earth. He'd cursed God, and yet here he was, walking up and down on this migrant earth. No, that earth wasn't going to eat anybody, and not *him*. And that went for the sun, too. No sun was going to eat *him*. No sir.

Wide awake, past surprise, awe, shock, he got up; up and off to the fields as before. As always, a cool fresh-aired morning. Nothing new. With clouds, too. But it wasn't yesterday any longer. He felt, he knew now that he could do what he wanted to. That he could do anything, could undo anything. Anything on this earth he wanted to. Yeah.

He looked at the plowed land, its dirt, that earth around him, and then—suddenly—he kicked it! Hard. As hard as he could now. And he said:

"No; not yet you don't. Not yet. You won't eat me, no. You're not getting *me* yet! Someday, but not today. No. And when you *do*, ha! I won't *care*; I won't even *know* . . ."

With This Ring

Do you remember a man called Don Laíto? Do you? You remember his wife? Doña Bonny? You do? Those weren't their real names, right? I mean, people called them that, but those weren't their names at all. Hilario was his name, and her's was Bonifacia. And I remember them, too; I'll say.

Well, one time, a long time ago, and I was just a kid then, I stayed with them at that place of theirs; and I stayed with them for three weeks, too. Enough for me to finish school that spring term, and it wasn't bad being with them; at first. Later on, well, later on, it wasn't so hot, let me tell you.

Oh, I know you used to hear all kinds of stuff about them, and about how they made bread, right? It was true, every word. A-course, people wouldn't mention the bread making to their faces, but d'you also remember how people'd say those two would rob you blind, and steal things? Well, that part was true, too. And I saw it all. First hand.

But they weren't exactly bad, see? I can't explain it, but let me say this: after I'd been there a while, about the same time school let out, I was getting kind of scared, see? Scared to ride around with them in that old car of theirs, afraid to stay one more night in that place where they lived, and afraid to eat their food, too. Know what I'd do then? I'd sneak off to some corner candy store, yeah, and stuff myself on candy. And I did this till my folks showed up—thank God they came by—till they came by to pick me up when they did.

As I said, the stay there started off pretty good: they were real nice to me that first day. Don Laíto'd laugh a lot, showing off the gold teeth, but I could make out the rotten ones, too. And his wife, Doña Bonny? Was she fat? Fatter'n fat, she was. And always hugging me until it got to be a pain after a while.

Boy, was she fat!

Well, that first meal was supper, but I was the only one who ate anything. They did without, or at least I think they did. Come to think, I don't know when they ate. I never saw them eating, anytime.

Anyway, she puts this piece of meat in the frying pan, and that meat looked kind-a green. Yeah. And smelled some, too. At first it smelled bad, really bad, but then the smell kind of wore off, okay? Maybe I got used to it; at any rate, Don Laíto he opened a window when she was cooking; had to. But I was hungry, and most of it tasted pretty good, so I ate it. Ate the whole thing, the smelly parts, too. Didn't want to hurt their feelings, see?

It seemed like everybody liked them, and that went for the Texas Anglos, too. The Texas Anglos'd give 'em canned goods and clothes, toys, too. Now, Don Laíto and Doña Bonny, they'd usually sell that stuff to us, but to show you what kind of folks they were, they'd give the stuff away, too, provided they couldn't sell it.

Sometimes you'd see them out in the fields, selling that bread they'd make, and they'd also sell thread, needles, stuff like that. Sometimes cans of this or that, sweet cactus, the kind you can eat with eggs, right? . . . and shoes, yeah. And coats, if they had them. Lots of stuff, and some of it was good. Not all, sure, but you know what I mean . . .

They'd say: "Look at this. Here's a nice pair of work shoes for you. They're a good buy, eh? A-course they're used, but so what? They're in good shape; here, look for yourself. This is quality footwear, this is. Wear like iron. You want a guarantee? Okay: these shoes here'll last you till they wear out. No kiddin'."

Like I said, I didn't want to hurt their feelings, so I wound up eating all the meat that first meal. All of it, but it must've not settled right 'cause I spent a lot of time in and out of the bathroom that first night. But that's not the best part: I hadn't seen my bedroom yet!

And you should've seen it! Well, you couldn't, there being no light, see? It was jam-packed, tight and close, on account of the smell. Full of all kinds of stuff, boxes of God-knows-what, and empty bottles; old calendars, piles of clothes. And there was just the one door to the place. Windows? Sure, but you couldn't see them or out of them, either. I mean, with all that junk piled there? And piled higher'n high. Might as well have had no windows, for all the good they did.

That first night I slept off and on, but mostly I didn't sleep; mostly I dozed off and off, instead of off and on. You see, I was worried about a hole in the ceiling. Well, I was sure—that hole was like a sky light, okay?—anyway, I was sure that a spider'd drop on me from up there. And then there was that smell again. Everywhere. Whew! Rancid like. And dark? Hmmmmmmmmmmmm. Once, that first night, I must've woken up 'round midnight, but I must've gone back to sleep; like that, off and off, see? And, when I was awake, all I could see was that hole up there. Why, I even thought I could see faces up there; my imagination, sure, but what could I do?

But I was scared, whatever it was that was up there. So that did it as far as sound sleep was concerned. But I guess I must've slept some, and when I did, it was beginning to get light outside. At times, in my sleep, I guess, I thought I could see them, Don Laíto and Doña Bonny, sitting there 'round the bed, staring at me. I even reached out a couple of times, just to make sure. I don't mind telling you, I wanted to go home, I wanted Pa to come for me, now, right away. Something in my bones, in my heart. Like something was bound to happen. But don't get me wrong. It's not that they weren't nice to me, they *were*. But like people said: You got to watch 'em. Close like.

School was something else entirely. I was getting along all right; the classes were going pretty good, but it was the going home, to those two.

Say, ah, say I'd come home of an afternoon and that little house'd be quiet. Spooky. Not a sound, uh-huh. But Doña Bonny, well, she'd choose the quietest time, see? And then: She'd scare me half to death. And she'd *laugh*? Shoot. Me, jumping about ten feet down the line, and you know what she'd do then? She'd laugh harder. Yeah. She'd laugh herself silly sometimes. Oh, I'd laugh, too, at first. Later on, though I didn't think it was so durn funny. Later on it got to where I hated it; but you think she'd stop? Ha!

And then, about a week later, been there a week, they started dropping hints. Hints about what they did when they went on into town. In the stores there. Know what? They'd steal! What? Most anything, anything that wasn't nailed down: food, liquor, clothing, cigarettes. Meat. Yeah. And then they'd go out and sell the stuff, but again—and that's why it's hard to make them out—what they couldn't sell, they'd give away. They'd even deliver the stuff to somebody's door for 'em. See?

But this next part is really awful. They told me I could come watch 'em bake pan de dulce, that Mexican bread; store-bought type. Pan de dulce. And old Don Laíto, he'd first take off his shirt, and he always looked sticky to me, somehow. And when he worked the dough, a big pile of it, he'd run up a sweat. And, while he worked the dough—while he was at it—he'd bring both his hands up to those hairy, sweaty armpits of his. Yeah, and *then* (and he didn't wipe them or anything) and then he'd bring both hands right into the dough. Aagh! But it was true, what people said about them. So he'd be watching me, see? He knew what he was doing, and there I was, rolling my eyes and I'd get kind of nauseous. He'd laugh, that's all. Yeah. And smiling right at me, the whole time. And he'd say, "*All* the bakers do that." Ugh.

I'm here to tell you I didn't take bite one out-a that pan

de dulce he made. No sir. And there'd be piles of it, all over the house. Well, thank-you-kindly-but-no-thanks.

And then, one day, right after school, they wouldn't let me in the house. Know what they did instead? They put me to work in their backyard. Now, the work wasn't all that hard, but it was the *idea* of it: workworkwork. Do this, do that; *you* know. And at all hours, too. Kind of screwy. But what the heck, my Pa'd paid them! Pa paid 'em my room and board. I don't have to work, I'd say to myself. I was going to school, that was my *job*, Pa'd said. But that didn't matter to them. It just got worse when they took me to town.

Ha! Grab that five-pound sack of flour, they'd say. Is that crazy? Stealing? But I wouldn't do it, and I didn't. It wasn't right; no sir. Well, Don Laíto he'd laugh: "You ain't cut out for this; you ain't got the guts for it. Man needs balls for that," he'd say.

And it didn't get any better; I was more than ready to leave. Run away. Yeah, I considered that too. But what could I do? Pa'd left me there with those two, and he'd already paid them his hard earned money. Yeah.

And let's not talk about the food again. The work? Oh, they kept me at it. And then . . .

Look. I'm about to tell you something, but this story stays here. You 'n me? Okay? Shake on it, now.

It started off with the Wetback. A wetback, see? No, I don't know his name. I started noticing a pattern of some kind. The Wetback he'd come calling but only when Don Laíto wasn't home. Now, how did the Wet know that? Anyway, whatever it was, say I was inside the house doing some work for them, okay? Well, Doña Bonny she'd sort of push me out and then she'd *bolt* the door. But say I was already outside, well, then she'd just lock me out. Just like that, and out I'd stay, too. Oh, yeah.

Doña Bonny once started to tell me what it was she did, what was going on between her and the Wet, but, I . . . I . . .

I didn't want to hear about that. I was embarrassed, see? But she went ahead and talked about it anyway, but I sure let my mind wander when she did. I just flat didn't want to know about such things.

But the Wet, he'd pass her money, I learned. The Wet was an old looking guy. But he'd smarten up some and use after shave stuff. And when he'd leave, you could still smell whatever it was he was using.

And then, one night, I heard something . . . Don Laíto first. And then Doña Bonny. They were whispering. Talking in that quiet house.

"I know what I'm telling you, this guy's got money holed up somewhere. What relatives? What-are-you-talking-about? He ain't got any relatives. Not here anyway. Look, Laíto, it'd be easy. Like taking candy, you get me? And who's he got here? Nobody."

"You sure, Bonny?"

"That man he works for doesn't know what's going on, and you think he cares about the Wetback? Ha! That's why he hired him in the first place. So *what* if something happened to him? Who's to know? You really think that grower's gonna worry about one more wetback? About a *mojado*, a wet-back?"

"Yeah, I guess you're right . . . No one knows he comes around here, right?"

"Who's to know? Look, you just leave all of this to me, Laíto."

"Like taking candy, eh?"

"You just leave that to me."

So, that very next day, right after school again, I went out . . . was sent out to the backyard. They laid out some lines on the ground and marked 'em off. A square. Dig, they said. It's going to be a root cellar, they said. Take your time, but don't dawdle, they said. Preserves, they said. Doña Bonny's gonna jar-up some stuff for us.

Hmmmmmmmph. I went at it, though. Three days straight of that digging, and then they told me to stop, to hold it right there. I thought the pit was kind of shallow for a cellar.

Changed their minds, they said.

But now listen to this: and I want you to know I remember it like it was just this morning. No kidding. I really do. That old man he showed up that afternoon; he'd got himself a haircut and he smelled up the place like he always did. So, I was locked out again, right? That Wet he stayed there a long time; the sun started going down by the time Doña Bonny called me in.

For supper, she says. And then guess what? Don Laíto he was already there! Inside! Now, how did he do that?

Well, I ate my supper and they said: "Off to bed you go. Hurry, now." It was early, but into that smelly old bedroom I went.

Talk about a fright! A fright to end 'em all. I was in bed, and I thought it was a snake! In the bed, hear? Know what it was? The Wetback! His arm! I thought he was drunk then, passed out. I jumped out-a that bed and lit out through that door, and from there, to the *kitchen*.

That old couple was fit to be tied. Laugh? I thought they'd never stop. And then? Well, that's when I saw the blood. The Wet's blood! On my shirt front. Sopping red. Man-oh-man, I didn't know *what* to say, think . . . And then I saw Don Laíto's teeth, he was smiling at me . . . And I saw the gold. And the rot, too. Oh, I remember that . . .

So they waited until it got dark, and me with them. Nothing to do but to help them drag out the body. Can you imagine that? Me? A kid? Well, they made me do it, forced me, made me help them. And you know where we took him to? Hmph. To that hole I'd started, that's where!

I didn't much want to, right? But you got to know what it was that those two told me: "We'll tell the cops *you* did it."

You beat that? All I thought about was my dad's money—how he'd paid these two—and then I thought about the Anglos—how much they liked these two. And then what all my dad had wanted me to do was to finish school someday. Finish school and get myself a nice little job somewhere. Nothing like their job out in the field and in the sun all day, see? And here I was, with these two.

But, I went ahead and helped them; laid the Wet in that hole and then the three of us began to cover him up. I didn't even see his face; ever. All I wanted now was to get out of there, to finish school, have my folks come for me . . . That was all I wanted, and I wanted it now.

Two weeks to go, and those were the longest in any-body's history. But I also thought I'd forget this somehow. In time. I'd forget, I kept saying. But no; no such thing. The next day, Don Laíto was already wearing the Wet's wrist-watch, right where I could see it. And out in the backyard? Well, there was this hump of dirt, see?

Finally. When my folks drove in, the first thing they said was, "You look kind-a skinny, boy. You sick or something?"

And I lied. Naw, I'm all right, I said. I just play a lot here and at school . . .

So, right before I left, Don Laíto and Doña Bonny both came up and gave me a hug, yeah. And then they made a big to-do and all. And then, in a whisper (but loud enough for Pa to hear) they said I'd better not say a word to anyone, 'cause if I did, they'd call the police. Like a game we were all playing, see? And they laughed and laughed, like I told you.

And my dad? Oh, he thought it was a great-big-huge joke, see?

So we drove off, Pa, Ma, my two kid brothers and me; back to where my Pa worked, and he and Ma talked about Don Laíto and Doña Bonny, and about how everybody liked them.

All I did was to look out the window of the pickup truck. Oh, I'd nod in agreement once in a while. Yeah. Nice folks.

Two months'd gone by, and I was well on the way to forgetting parts of what had happened back there when both of them showed up. For a visit. They'd come all the way out here, to this farmland Pa was working then. And they'd brought me a present, they said.

A ring.

And then there was nothing I could do *but* take it. Try it on, they said. Put it on, they said. Hmph. I knew whose ring it was, right away. The Wet's.

And then, just as soon as they left, I wanted to get rid of it; bury it; dump it somewhere . . .

But I didn't. I couldn't. I can't even tell you myself why I didn't, couldn't. Fear, most likely, right? The fear that someone would find it, right?

But that's not the worse of it. It goes on, see? 'Cause then, for a long time after that, I'd look up, see a stranger somewhere, and the first thing I'd do was to run the ring hand down my front pants pocket. And I'd keep it there; keep it there long after the stranger had gone, disappeared . . .

And that was a habit that stayed, lived with me for a long time. A long time. Yeah.

Devil With Devil Damn'd

There was this full moon out, see? . . . and he'd decided by then to call out the Devil. Dare him, sort of. And it was clear; star-studded. Silvery, almost. One of those bright nights you can almost read by. You know the kind. And there was a whiff of daylight about it, it was so bright.

Now, going out at night to call the Devil, well, that was something he'd been thinking about for a long time, but he'd just decided on it that day. Naturally enough, he had a fear on, but this soon gave way to fear's sister: curiosity. And there was some doubt, too: what would happen if he went through with this idea of his? *Could* something happen if he went through with it?

Eventually, though, curiosity shoved fear aside, and that was that.

When night came and his father turned off the light in that one-room chicken coop they were staying in, he knew he was going out. That night, at midnight. The best time, he said. Now, he'd just inch over to that door there, sliding and gliding, and then right up to the door with nobody feeling or hearing or seeing him. Had to be tonight.

"Pa, aren't you going to leave the door open for us? There's no mosquitos out, right?"

"I know that, but I'm thinking about the animals, son. A rat or something. You remember what happened over to the Flores's coop that time? One a-them coons, a ring tail, it snuck up in there with them, 'member?"

"Sure, but that was a couple of seasons ago, Pa. C'mon, what do y'say? Leave it open just a bit, okay? It's still kind-a hot, Pa. Besides, what could come in here? There's a clump a-trees out there, but that's for grackles, and they sure won't come in no chicken coop, right? The rest of the people with us leave their's open . . ."

"Yeah, and they do that 'cause *they* got screen doors aside from the wooden ones, see? We don't."

"Not all a-them, they don't. Go on, Pa . . . look at that moon! Isn't it pretty? Peaceful looking, ain't it?"

"All right, all right."

"What's the boy going on about now?"

"Nothing; he's all right. He just wants the door open, that's all. I'll go ahead and open it a crack."

"You going to leave the door open?"

"Just a tad, okay? Don't *you* start worrying; nothing's going to happen."

The Devil—the very idea of a *Devil*—this had fascinated him for a long time; he couldn't even remember when he didn't think about the Devil.

And recently, it had been on his mind even more, and way before Aunt Pana's Christmas *pastorelas*, those Christmas plays with Baby Jesus, the Devil, and the shepherds, and everything. Before that, yeah. And before something else, too: before he'd discovered Old Man Lightning's—Don Rayos', remember him?—well, before he discovered that costume of his. The Devil's own with that big, black cape, and the smoky tin mask he wore, and the horns, too. The boy'd had stumbled across the whole outfit under Don Rayos's house a time he was playing there. He saw that mask, the cape; everything. You see, he'd dropped a shooter, an aggie or a taw, and it'd rolled under the house, and there they were for all the world to see: the horns, that shiny black cape and mask . . . the whole shebang, yeah! And then he'd dragged it out from under the house. Full a-dust it was; him, too. The boy then shook off the dust, and then he went ahead and put on the mask; yeah.

"The way I look at it, Compadre, Man just wasn't meant to fool around with the Devil or with the Devil's things, either. I've even heard of men who've called out to him, oh yes. I can tell you that right now. A-course, some go out in a group, see?

"Try to lessen the fear that way, but the Devil's not about to show his face then. No sir. Know what he does? He waits. Yeah, sure; waits until he gets 'em one-by-one, all alone. And *that's* how the Devil works it. And you know what? He doesn't always *look* like the Devil, that's right.

"I know what I'm talking about here. No, sir, a man can't afford to get mixed up with the Devil no way . . . And here's something else, too: say you do meet up with him. Ha! He's got your soul right then and there, ah-hah. And then comes the shock and fright, and people die a-that. No, not all of 'em, but some. First off, they get kind-a sad-like, and then they stop talking all together, yessir. Why, it's like their very soul has left them . . . flown away, you might say."

The boy, lying on the floor as he was, could make out the clock easily enough; he was just waiting for his chance. The two kid brothers were the first to go to sleep, and all he was waiting for was his folks to drop off.

On either side of him stood the chicken coops where the other fieldhands slept, entire families, just like his. And he could hear the snoring coming across the way, but it was the time which dragged by. For that clock to move from eleven to 11:55 was like a year to him. And as he lay there—with that clock ticking away—he'd change his mind, but then he'd look outside again, and it was nice, quiet, and clear. The moon saw to that.

And he thought:

"Now. Say I leave here at ten to midnight, that'll give me time enough to reach that clump a-trees there, the grove. Be right in the middle of 'em. Mmmmmmmmm; it's a good thing there's no snakes hereabouts . . . I'd sure hate to run into *them* out there in the middle a-that grove there . . . And in those *weeds*, too.

"Here's what I'll do: I'll call him at twelve on the dot. Right at twelve. But I'd better take that clock with me just to make sure a-the time, 'cause you got to call him at the right time. If you don't, he won't show up, and that's it. Twelve midnight, and it's got to be at twelve sharp, right on the nose, or there's nothing doing . . . not eleven fifty-nine, no sir. Twelve. On the button."

First thing he did was to get his hands on that table clock. Slow and easy now. And he was outside. Didn't make a sound. From this, he placed the clock in his pants pocket, and he could hear the ticking. Loud. He started walking away from the chicken coops as carefully and as quietly as he could. And then, all of a sudden, he stopped. Just checking. It was nothing, but he thought someone was watching him all the same. Yeah, but who?

And on he went, and just as quiet, too. Past the outdoor privies and beyond them now. Looking back, he could see he was a good distance away from the chicken coops where his folks slept. He figured he was far enough away now, and talking softly to himself, he said:

"And how does it go, now? Right. I'll call and, but what if he appears there, sudden-like? No; no, I don't think he'd do *that*, just like that.

"But what if he does? Well, so what? What can he do to me? I'm not dead yet . . . So, just as long as I'm alive, there's nothing he *can* do. It's just that . . . I just want to know, for myself. That's all. *Is* there a Devil or not?

"Okay. Say there's *no* Devil. *And* if there's no Devil, maybe there's no G . . . uh-huh . . . better not say *that*. I mean, I could be punished, right? Let me put it this way: if there's no Devil, then maybe there's no punishment either. No, that can't be right 'cause you gotta have punishment and suffering.

"Okay, now how am I going to call him? Do I just say *Devil*, is that it? How about if I call him Old Hornie? Or Ketch . . . *Jack* Ketch. Old Nick. Clootie. Lucifer. Satan . . . Well, whatever comes out first, that's what I'll use."

And he arrived at the grove and walked deeper into it. And then he stood there. The words wouldn't come out, see? There was fear there, but then, just-like-that, accidental-like, the words popped out. But nothing happened. And he wasn't whispering either. So, he called him again, and he used all those names: Ned. Nick. Clootie. Old Hornie.

Nothing. At all. Why, everything looked the same, *was* the same. Just like it'd been a few minutes before. Peace and quiet.

But he wasn't through yet. Next thing to do was to swear, yeah, cuss him out. And then he did this, too. Nothing happened. So up he came with all the cuss words he knew, and he'd even use different tones of voice, too. Nothing.

He then cursed the Devil's mother, yeah, that'll bring him out. Cussed her, *then* cussed *him*. Nothing. Not-a-thing, see?

And nothing had changed, no one had appeared. Everything was the same. Just like an hour ago; thirty minutes ago; *now*.

He made for home, to bed.

What a disappointment; and after all a-that, too. Ah, but now he felt like a man: tough, mean. Brave, too; yeah, he did. The wind went right through the leaves, shaking them, making them dance some, sounding off some. And he could feel the faint breeze now.

No such thing as the Devil. Nope. Nothing. The wind was the only thing with him here, and he headed for the coops. . . .

"Okay, if there's no Devil, does that mean that there's no . . . but what am I saying? I better watch that kind-a talk. I could be punished for it. Yeah, I could. But one thing's sure: there's no such thing as a Devil anywhere.

"Maybe, and I mean just *maybe*, like in it-could-be-just-perhaps-maybe . . . Nah! If there was a Devil, he would've come out by now. Sure he would've; it's just that there's no such thing, that's all.

"I mean, like tonight, right? That was the perfect time. Right? So what happened? Nothing. Midnight. Me. All alone. Calling him. Hah! There's no Devil. No sir."

A couple of times there he thought he heard his name being called out. But he wouldn't turn around. Wouldn't look back. What for? Why should I, he'd say. There's nothing there—and it wasn't 'cause he was afraid, either. It was nothing. Nobody.

And then he was there, home; the chicken coops. Quietly, he got down on the floor, and the Devil wasn't there either. Lying on the floor, eyes open, and then came a slight shiver, and he felt queasy-like. Must've been the strain of it all, don't you see? Something he ate.

But he didn't even try to go to sleep just yet. He wanted to think some. Needed to.

"There's no Devil. Nothing. There's no Devil and no nothing to go with it. No sir."

His voice—*that*—that was the only thing out there, in that clump a-trees. Nothing else. And then he thought about how right the people had been! Sure. They were right when they said you just didn't go around playing with the Devil— the devil.

Clear as anything. Those people who called out to him; to the devil, those who sought him out and went crazy. Well, they went crazy not because he appeared, but because there's no such thing. No devil. None.

They went crazy because the devil didn't appear. To them. To anybody. That's why, and that's why he didn't appear, he *couldn't*. Hmph.

Hardest thing to remember, to know, even, is that moment when one falls asleep. Can't be done. The boy looked out into the night; clear, bright. And there was the moon again. Beaming. Happy about something; skipping, sliding, and gliding right through the clouds it was.

The Hurt

It's the hurt; that's why I hit him back and just as hard as I could, too. But what am I going to do now?

Maybe—just maybe, now—maybe I wasn't really kicked out of school. I mean, maybe it didn't happen; maybe I misheard the principal. Right?

Naw, they kicked me out, all right. I'll say they did. But . . . but what am I going to *do*? About home?

I think I know when it all started. I was shamed, and ashamed, too, but mostly, mostly I was just angry. Both, together, at the same time . . . Oh me, I sure don't want to go home now. And what am I going to say to Ma, anyway? And then? Well, Pa'll come in from the cropfield, and I'll catch it from both of them then. And a good belting into the bargain. But—well, you just get fighting mad, and there's the shame, and anger, too. It's the hurt.

Durn! Happens every time we come Up North to these schools. Yeah. They just stare at you. Up and down. And then they laugh; and right to your face, too. And that school teacher . . . In she comes with that Eskimo Pie stick a-hers. Looking for lice and cooties, she says.

Shoot! Anyone'd be embarrassed at that. Right there: in front of everybody else. But that's not all of it, 'cause then they turn their noses up at you, and that brings on the anger. It's bound to; can't they see that?

Best thing for me to do is to stay out in the fields; out-a everybody's way. Out by that grove there, the one near the chicken coops. Yeah, the fields, that's where. But anywhere'll do me, really. Anywhere; free.

"Look alive, son; we're almost there."

"And you'll come in with me this time, Pa? To register?"

"Nah. You don't need me. Really. I mean, you speaking English and all, right? See that door, that must be the main entrance. Now, if you don't know where to go exactly, just ask somebody, anybody. Right. Don't hang back now; you go in and ask somebody. Nothing to it, boy; and there's nothing to be afraid of, either."

"Yeah . . . but why won't you . . . why don't you come in with me, Pa?"

"You don't need *me*, son. Hey? You're not scared, are you? Good . . . Go on; that's got to be the main door. See it? Look, there's someone coming up there now—a man, see? Now: best behavior, okay?"

"Sure, Pa . . . But can't you . . . can't you help me out, Pa? Register with me?"

"Oh, you'll do right well without me; I'd only be in your way. Go on—nothing to be afraid of. Right?"

It's the same thing every time. First they take you to see the nurse, and right off she starts checking you for lice. Yeah, and it's all those old ladies' fault too. A-course it is. Come a Sunday, and there they go, out in the sun, right by the chicken coops where everybody'll see them. And what do they *do*? They start combing their hair, checking for lice. Out in the open! But what about the Anglo men and their wives, huh? What do they do? Well, come a Sunday they drive out there where we're staying. They drive up and they point their fingers at us, at those old ladies.

Pa's right; Pa says that when those old ladies start delousing themselves, they begin to look like monkeys out in a zoo somewheres. But what the heck, they give us chicken coops to live in, and who wants to live with lice, anyway?

"Here, Ma, hold it, let me tell you this: I was barely in the classroom, okay? Just sat down and then I was sent back out again: Go see the nurse, they said. And there *she* was, all in white.

"First off, she made me take my clothes off; all of them. Stripped naked I was, and she looked at my behind. Yeah. But it was my head she was really interested in. Sure she was; but I was all cleaned up, right? You think that mattered to that nurse? Hmph! Know what she did? I'll tell you: she brought herself one a-those jars full a-vaseline, it looked like. And it stunk! Worm killer it smelled like . . . can you still smell it on me, Ma?

"Well, she rubbed it in—clean head or not. And it itched, too. Then she picked up a pencil, yeah she did. And she began parting my hair with it. Hmph. And then? Get dressed, she says, and I do, and I go right back to class.

"But I felt bad; ashamed, Ma. Of myself, see? And, and . . . And they made me *strip*, Ma. Shirt, pants, and my shorts, too. Yes'm, right in front of that old nurse."

And now? What am I going to tell my folks when I get home? That I was kicked out? Expelled? No . . . But . . . but it wasn't all my fault. Not all of it; not entirely. That Anglo boy, he looked like trouble, right off. He just stared, but no laughter out-a him; staring, looking right at me, and then I was sent off—to sit by myself, yeah. Away from everybody else . . . and that Anglo boy? He kept his eyes on me; shot me the finger, too. Yes, he did.

But the hurt was something else; being set apart like

103

that. Why, everybody had a clear shot at me. And they stared, and then *I* felt like a monkey in the zoo. A-course I was angry, but I was embarrassed; embarrassed by being set apart, away from the rest of the class.

And then, when it came to my turn to read, I didn't. Or I couldn't. It felt funny, though: I could *hear* myself all right, but the words, the words weren't coming out at all. Strange . . .

Hmmm. This is a nice cemetery . . . nothing scary about this one; not a bit. It's pretty. Go right across it every day, to and from school. Green. And nice. The grass is leveled off, too, why, parts of it are paved! Looks like a golf course or something . . .

But I won't be playing here today; no rolling down that little hill there; no somersaulting, either; and, I won't have a chance to lie down on the grass today; not for long, anyway. Lie down, listen, try to count the different sounds I hear . . . counted up to twenty-six of them the last time I was here . . .

Now, if I hurry, I might just be able to run into doña Cuquita, maybe go on to the City Dump with her. Yeah, that's what I'll do. She usually starts out about this time when the sun's cooling down some.

"Careful, kids . . . watch your step now; some of this stuff's on fire, even if you can't see it. And you can't tell just by looking. Careful, I said. Might be some coals smouldering down there. I know what I'm talking about: I got me a good burn once, and I got the scar to prove it . . . Here, kids. Here, look, each one of you grabs a long pole and you poke it about, okay? But you got to poke hard. There.

"Now, that old dump Inspector shows up, you just tell him you came to *leave* stuff. He's all right—most of the time—he mostly looks for those little books, the dirty kind.

Never mind him now.

"Oh, and keep an eye out when we're up on that trestle there . . . Man was run over last year some time. Got caught right in the middle of the trestle there, and he tried to outrun the train."

"Do all you kids have your folks' permission to be out here with me? Do you? Now, don't be eating anything less you wash it first, okay?"

Okay. Let's say doña Cuquita shows up, then what? If I do go with her—and without permission—that's a belting, for sure. But what am I going to tell 'em at home about school? Well, maybe they really didn't go through with it, maybe they didn't kick me out.

What am I saying? *A-course they did.*

But what *can* I say? That it wasn't *all* my fault? And that I just had to go real bad, and then when I did, that same Anglo boy was right there, right by that urinal—that same Anglo boy, giving me looks and stares, and a hard time, too. Yeah.

"Hey, Mex . . . I don't like Mexicans because they steal. You hear me?"

"Yes."

"I don't like Mexicans. You hear, Mex?"

"Yes."

"I don't like Mexicans because they steal. You hear me?"

"Yes."

I remember the first fight I had in school. Back home. And I was scared, too, and it had all been arranged, planned out ahead of time by the big guys. Why, some a-those second graders were big enough to grow a mustache, yeah, they were. And the fight was all their doing, too. They kept shoving me and that other boy together, against each other. Yeah. I guess we fought more out-a fear than anything else. The fight started just a block away from school; those older boys started pushing Ramiro and me, and like I said, we fought each other, too. Real hard. Lucky for us two neighbor ladies came out and separated the both of us. And *then*, after the fight, I thought I was pretty tough. Hmph . . . but I was plenty scared right up to the time of the fight, though.

But it was different this time around. No warning; nothing. That boy just hauled off and whacked me one behind the ear. Hard, too. Things sounded kind-a hollow for me, like at the beach, when you bring a shell up to your ear or something . . . I don't even remember hitting that guy, but I must've 'cause someone went for the principal: There's a fight in the boys' room!

It wasn't all my fault, so . . . maybe I didn't get kicked out, after all.

Fat chance a-that. I was kicked out. Period.

And how'd that principal hear about the fight, anyhow? I mean, who went and told him? That janitor . . . eyes popping out-a his head. *He* was scared, all right, and him holding that broom ready to whack me one. . . . sure he was. Ready to give me what-for, he was; ready and willing, he was.

"The Mexican kid just got in a fight and beat up a couple of our boys . . . No, not bad . . . but what do I do?"

. . . .

"No, I guess not, they could care less if I expel him . . . They need him in the fields."

. . . .

"Well, I just hope our boys don't make too much about it to their parents. I guess I'll just throw him out."

. . . .

"Yeah, I guess you're right."

. . . .

"I know you warned me. I know . . . I know . . . but . . . yeah, okay."

And where did that janitor think I was going to run off to, anyway? Everyone at home wants me, *expects* me to stay in school . . . and besides, that janitor, he kept waving that big old broom at me. He just stood there, watching, ready for anything,. . . And then, it was over, kicked out, they said. Leave, they said. Go on home.

Home!

This part of the cemetery puts me halfway to home. It's sure a pretty one, though. Nothing like the one back home, in Texas. That one'll really scare you. I just can't get used to it. And you know what really scares me about the cemetery at home? It's the funerals, or after the funerals, anyway. I look up and there's an old archway with writing on it. *Forget Me Not*, it says. Yeah. It's like I can hear the dead. Talking. Saying those words to me. And the words stay—stick—yeah. Why, even I don't look up at the archway, the words just come right at me. It doesn't matter, you don't even have to look at them, the words. They're there.

But not here; this is a nice cemetery—grass, trees, real nice. And I guess that's why the people here don't cry much at funerals. Too pretty to cry in. And I can play in it, too. Be great if we could fish here, though; be easy, too. But I, we, can't fish here; need a license for that, and besides, they wouldn't sell fishing licenses to *us*; we're from out of state.

And now, I won't be able to go to school anymore. And

what is it I'm going to tell them at home? I can't remember how many times I've been told that the teachers are our second parents . . . And *now* what?

And, and, and when we all get back to Texas? What then? Why, everybody'll know. Sure they will. Ma and Pa're going to get angry—I know they are. I'll get that belting sure, now. Maybe more than just the belt, too.

And to top it off, my uncle—and my grandfather, too—they're *all* going to find out. If I'm not careful, why, I could maybe land in one a-those state schools they're always talking about. They'll sure straighten you out there, in those places. Quick. Take the starch right out-a one, there. Go in like a lion, come out like a lamb. Yessir.

But . . . it's possible, kind-a; maybe they *didn't* kick me out. Maybe, I left too soon . . .

Who'm I kidding? Still, it's just poss . . . forget it: I'm *out*.

Now, I could make out like I went to school every day. Sure. But instead, I'd stay here, in the cemetery. Yeah. I could do that. But how about later on? What *then*? Well, I *could* say that I lost my report card. Sure, that's it.

But that's the least of it; what really hurts is that I won't ever get to be a telephone operator, like my Dad wants, 'cause that's what Pa wants me to study for . . . but . . . but, ah, you got to finish school for that job.

"Hon! *Vieja*—woman—call the boy out . . . Compadre, ask the boy here what it is he wants to do—what he wants to be—when he grows up and is out of school."

"Well, what's it going to be, godson?"

"I'm not sure."

"Sure you are! Go on! Tell him! Don't hang back, the man's your godfather, after all."

"What's it going to be, *ahijado*? What do *you* want to do?"

"I want to be a telephone operator."

"Do you, now?"

"Yes, he does. Compadre, he has his heart set on it; he really does. Every time we talk about this, he says he wants to be a telephone operator. And I imagine the pay's pretty good, don't you? And just the other day, I told my Boss himself about this, but all he did was laugh. Hmph. Probably figures my boy's not up to it—well, he's wrong there, I'll tell you; he doesn't know my boy like I do, and that's a fact. The boy's smart as a whip. And that's why he goes to school. I don't ask God for much, but this I do, I want my boy to finish school; I want him to make something out of himself. Know what I mean, Compadre? Make something out of himself: a telephone operator."

That was some movie, that was. And the telephone operator, why, he had the most important job of all . . . I think that's why Pa's so set on it once I finish school . . .

But, you know . . . it's still possible; maybe I wasn't expelled just like that. I mean, what if it didn't happen?

What am I going to *do*? Well, one thing's sure: no one'll have to ask me what it is I'm going to do when I grow up now.

But, you know, it just could be. An outside chance. NO! What am I saying? I was there. A fact's a fact, and the fact is I was booted out. But the hurt!

The hurt, the shame; both, together. Best thing for me is to stay put right here. But then, what about Ma? She'll be scared, stiff; scared just like when there's lightning and thunder and all. She gets scared to death . . .

No, no, no . . . I've just *got* to tell them. Got to. And now, when Godfather comes calling, I, I, I guess I'm going to have to hide off somewheres. But then I won't get a change to read for him any more, the way Pa always likes me to. I know what I'll do on Godfather's next visit: I'll run and hide behind the cedar chest; maybe under the bed, even. And *that'll* avoid embarrassment all around . . . Yeah.

But won't it be something? If they didn't really kick me out? I mean, maybe it's all been a big mistake. Won't it be something, though? I mean, who can tell? Right? Maybe I haven't been kicked out, after all.

Hmph . . . *A-course I have* . . .

First Fruits

Midspring meant first communion, and that was the priest's, the Father's, doing, his schedule.

First communion day, mine; can anyone not remember their first?

I remember what we all wore (white) and what I had for late breakfast: hot chocolate and pan de dulce, that sweet bakery-bought bread. This last was also a rite, for after communion.

And I also remember the tailor shop, and what I saw there. The tailor shop stood to the side and across the street from the parish church, and I saw what I saw because I got to church early. Earlier than anybody else, in fact. And I got there early because I couldn't sleep; and I couldn't sleep because of the sins; I mean because of the exact number of sins I had to confess to. All of us had to remember each and every sin and then to keep track of how many we'd committed and what kind, too, so we'd come up with the right total.

And I'll tell you why else I couldn't sleep. There was a scary picture Ma'd placed on the wall at the foot of the bed. And too, the room had been repapered, and I could see ghosts in that new pattern. And then that picture Ma'd hung up was a picture of Hell; the real thing; yeah. So there I was: first communion and how may sins was it? And Hell. And the ghosts on the wall paper. Everything jumbled up together.

"Now, boys and girls, you must please stop that squirming. Quiet now. Ready? One: you've all got your prayers down, and this is good. Two: you know which sins are mortal and which are not. Fine. Three: you know what a sacrilege is. Right? Four: we're all of us God's own children. Yes. And, five: although we're in God's grace, we can always lose it, and when this happens, the Devil will then claim us as his children—pay attention. And we don't want this."

"Next. When it's your turn at the confessional, you must account for your sins—mortal or venial—and you must account for all of them. And you know why? Well, because if you don't confess all . . . if you leave one out and then go ahead and take *la hostia*, the host, what will that be? A sacrilege. Right! And when one commits a sacrilege, what happens? Well? Right, we're Hell bound. And don't forget: God knows everything. Everything we do, everything we think.

"You can lie to me, the Sister, and get away with it; why, you can even lie to Father, but you can't lie to God. God knows everything. Everything . . .

"And another thing: you have to be pure in spirit and cleansed of sins; if not, then there's no communion for you. You shouldn't go up to the railing and take communion. That's a sacrilege.

"And one thing more: You must start thinking on your sins now. Each-and-everyone-of-them. How would you feel if you took communion and then remembered you had left one out, forgot one of them?

"Fine, fine . . . Let's run over the sins again. And we'll start with the sins of the flesh, the things we do when we touch ourselves, our bodies. Who's going to go first?"

I remember that Sister always started off on sins of the flesh, but the truth is I didn't understand what she really meant then. And besides that, we practiced the part about the sins of the flesh all the time. For me, Hell was the scary part. I'd stumbled into a brazier a short while back and got a good burn from that, so I knew all about Hell. And I also knew what Sister meant when she talked about Hell Everlasting. But I didn't know the other part: the part she liked, the sins +f the flesh part."

So there I was, the night before my first communion, counting all my sins: each-and-everyone-of-them. But that wasn't the hard part. The hard part was coming up with an actual number of them.

Dawn rolled by and I finally settled on something: I reckoned some one-hundred-and-fifty sins, but to be on the safe side, I was going to claim two-hundred; that would do it.

"The way I figure it, if I go ahead and confess to the one fifty, and then say I've left out some, by mistake, then I'll be in the wrong. Same as a sin. But if I say two hundred, even if I ain't done that many, it's more than one fifty, and that's not a sacrilege, right? Okay, so here's what I'm going to say: Bless me, Father, for I have sinned. 'How many sins?' 'Two hundred, Father. All kinds.' 'Anything else, the Commandments?' 'Them? Yes, Father. All ten, Father.'

"Sure, I'll just say all ten and in that way, I'm safe from sacrilege again. It's the best way, the more you claim, the cleaner you are. Yeah."

And I remember I got up early like I said, and earlier than usual, even for me. And Ma sure wasn't ready for that. Godfather was going to be waiting for me over at the church, and I sure didn't want to be late, not for a second.

"C'mon, Ma, hurry it up . . . you got to iron my pants,

okay? I . . . I thought you did that last night."

"No, I couldn't see a thing last night. There's something wrong with my eyes, they're getting weaker. I decided to do the ironing in the morning . . . but what's your hurry? You've got plenty of time. Confession's not till eight o'clock, isn't it? And what's it now? Six? Besides, your godfather won't get there until eight o'clock, that's the hour."

"Yeah, yeah, I know, but I couldn't sleep at all, Ma. Will you please hurry it up? I want to get going."

"All right, but tell me this: what're you going to be doing as early as all this?"

"It's just that I'm afraid I'm going to forget some sins, and I got to say 'em all to Father; I think it'll be easier if I'm inside the church. It's a help, see?"

"I'll be through here in a minute. You know, sonny, once my eyes start to clear up, I can go like sixty here."

So I headed for church, counting the sins one by one, keeping the sacraments in order, and like that. But there was hardly anybody around; the day was beginning to clear up and light was coming first here and then over there, but where was everybody? Maybe I *was* early, maybe Father slept late; maybe he was busy.

I then walked around just to be doing something, and I went by the side of the church and across the street to the tailor shop. Well! That's when I heard what sounded like people laughing, having a good time. But then I also heard some groans coming out of that tailor shop. Sounded like a neighborhood dog or something. But there went the voices again. And since I was sure it was voices, I peeked in, just for a second or so.

Two people, and I could see them clearly, but they hadn't seen me just yet. A man and a woman, and they weren't wearing clothes; and I saw them holding on to each other and rolling around some sheets and dresses, lying on the floor. I couldn't keep my eyes off them, and I remembered I didn't move away.

And then they saw me! They began to go after their clothes, yelling at me, telling me to get away from there. The woman must've been sick though; her hair was all mussed, and she didn't look too good. I started to run right then. To church I ran, but I kept thinking of them back there, and then that was all I could think of. And then it hit me: why, those must be the sins of the flesh Sister was always going on about, when we touch ourselves. Yeah.

And then it was back to thinking about those two back there; I could see them again even when I had my eyes closed. There they were, rolling on the floor. Naked.

The rest of the kids began to show up, gather around the church, and it was then I planned to tell them what I'd seen. Well, I planned to, but I didn't. I then decided to tell them later, after communion and everything. So, I didn't say a thing to 'em then. Or to anyone else, right? But I felt a kind of guilt. Guilty, like I'd done the sin of the flesh myself.

Too late to do anything about it now. And I sure couldn't tell the others, right? And I didn't. I didn't because if I had, why, they'd become sinners too, wouldn't they? Just like me. Yeah. (So . . . . Got it! I won't take communion, I won't take the host. And I won't go to confession either. But that's not right! I know about the sins of the flesh. I *know*, see? And I know what they mean. What Sister was going on and on about.)

But what if I don't go up front for communion? Well, both Pa and Ma'll know and everybody'll know. And Godfather, too. And I sure as shooting ain't going to leave Godfather at church, mouth hanging open, egg on his face like that. One choice and that's it: I got to confess what I just saw.

(And you know what? I got an itch to go back outside, to

see those two again. To see if they were still there. On the floor.)

Hold it! I got the one choice: I got to go straight to confession. But what if I lie, just a little bit? Or, what if I forget about what I saw, between now and confession time? Yeah, that's it. Better still, maybe I didn't see anything after all. Yeah. Sure. What I mean is, what if I didn't see anything? Well?

But there was no choice, was there? I *had* to go to confession, and I did. And I walked into that booth, I told Father I'd committed two-hundred sins, all kinds, too. I just left one out. I kept that one aside. I ate it. And then? And then I walked out of that confessional, and there was nothing to it.

Walked home with Godfather, and it was just like everything had changed somehow. But it looked smaller somehow. Less important, unimportant, it seemed to me.

And when we got home, there was Pa. And Ma, too. And I could see them on the floor. I really could. And then I looked around; all the grownups were naked. And they were all on the floor. And they were making all kinds of faces, too. Why, I could even hear them laughing. Oh, and then I saw Sister, too. Yeah. And she was on the floor . . .

But who could drink hot chocolate now? Or, eat the pan de dulce? But I had to, and I did, in a gulp, and then I rushed outside. Running hard. Away from the house, away from there, and away from them. I was choking and out of breath.

"Hey, what's wrong with that boy anyway? Running off like that? Where did he leave the manners we taught him, eh?"

"Aw, don't pay him no mind, Compadre, and don't worry about me. I know kids; I got some of my own, remember? I'll tell you something about kids nowadays: play is all they think about. All day long. But let him be: it's his first big day: Communion."

"Yeah, I guess you're right, Compadre. And it isn't as if I'm against him playing and all, but . . . well, you know how it is: they got to have some manners. Respectful, right? And they got to respect their elders 'cause we know better. And manners and respect to you as his godfather."

"No argument there about respect, Compadre. But you know how kids are."

I stopped running when I got to the *monte*, the boonies. And I was away from everybody, finally. Alone. By myself. Got me some rocks for target practice and I started on the cactus, and then I went after some of the bottles lying around. Broke them, too. I then shinnied up a pin oak, and stayed there a while till I got bored, and I'd climbed all the way to the top, too.

And then I thought back on the tailor shop. Yeah. And I liked it. Liked thinking about it. Oh, yeah. Heckfire, I even forgot I'd lied to Father at confession. Ha! And then? Then I remembered that traveling preacher, missionary I guess, and what he'd said about the grace of God and all.

And then, all of a sudden, I wanted to learn things. And I wanted to learn, period. More and more. A lot. And as I thought on this, it hit me that maybe everything was the same. Even after you did something, saw something. Everything. The same.

The Burden of the World

The fleas, that's what made him move around, squirm.
Under a house is where he was; and he'd been there for hours
it seemed. And he was in hiding. Early that morning, he'd
been on his way to school when, out of nowhere, the thought
struck him: skip. Skip school today. Now.

And he had. That old schoolteacher would take it out of
his hide, anyway; he hadn't learned the day's word list. From
this to going under the house was but a short, easy step.

But there was also a need, an urge to hide. Be off by
himself. Where? Anywhere. And for how long? It didn't matter. So, it was settled: he'd go off and hide somewhere, and
hang the time.

It was the dark that he liked, enjoyed it, in fact. But
those fleas! Bound to be spiders down here, too, but he went
ahead and crawled under the house, and there he stayed:
alone, comfortably alone and in secret.

Under the house. What daylight there was came off on a
straight line, about a foot from the ground. Face down, now,
his shoulders rubbing against the under boards, and these
gave him security somehow. But then the fleas got to him,
they forced him to move about, crawl about on his stomach; it
was that tight down there.

"If it weren't for the fleas. It's nice down here, and I bet
kids who play hookey regularly do this all the time; hide out
under some old house somewhere. No, not bad at all, and I
can think here. I mean, who's going to bother me down
here?"

Deep in thought, the fleas forgotten, and forgotten too that he was under a house. It was dark, safe, and he could think here; alone. Dark. The dark was necessary, to think in; and that's what he needed to do.

The first thought was that of his Pa telling him stories of witches and things. About how his Pa said he could charm owls off the trees; and he could too, with special prayers and with the seven knots to go with them. *That* would do it.

"Well, at that time we had some land of our own, and we had the watering rights to go with it. So, coming home and darkening some, it wasn't uncommon to see electric sparks, but more than sparks, they were round-shaped balls of fire. And these little balls would bounce up and down, around the telephone wires. From the city of Morelos down in Michoacan; that's where their home base was, that's where the witches lived. And one time, I almost got me one. Almost knocked one of those witches down.

"Old Don Remigio it was who taught me the prayers and the way to tie those special knots, too. First a prayer, then a knot, see? But you got to know what you're doing. Well, that time I almost got me one, I'd gone through all seven prayers and was working on the seventh knot. But you know what? I couldn't tie it. No different from the other knots, but I just couldn't tie it. I couldn't come up with it, but I was that close, see? And so close that the witch fell off the wire, landed at my feet, but it got up sudden-like. I just didn't have the last knot, see?"

". . . And that kid was so little, so young you know they don't understand so well at that age. And he couldn't hold off any longer; he was thirsty, and the water tank was there, at the edge of the row. Hmph. But I hear the guy's going scot free; he's got a lot of pull 'round here. But listen to this: how would it have been had we been the ones who shot one of their kids? What do you think would've have happened *then*? One of the things I heard was that the little kid's father had gone after a rifle, to even it up, see? But nothing came of it. Never could run into the guy, he said."

". . . That old lady? Sure, as soon as she'd set foot in the church, she'd start to cry, and then she'd be off into her prayers. And then, before she knows herself what she's doing, there she'd be, praying out loud, talking out loud. And then she'd start to wail, and scream, yeah, and moan some more. It was that son, don't you know. And if you didn't know her, you'd think she was having a fit or something . . ."

". . . You know who I think is still alive? Old Doña Cuquita; yeah. Been years since I've seen her, of course. She took good care of us out at that old dump. I really liked her. You know, I didn't get to know either of my grandmothers and neither did Pa, and maybe that's why he looked at her as a grandma . . . But like I said, I really liked Doña Cuquita, and I really liked it when she hugged me. Know what she'd say then? She'd say I was bright; brighter than the moon, she'd say."

"Get out of there, get away from that goddam window. Go away. Go away . . ."

". . . Nothing I can do, but you can't come home with me anymore. Look, I like to play with you, but some old ladies told Mama that Mexicans steal, and now Mama says not to bring you home anymore. You got to turn back. But we can still play at school. Okay? I'll choose you and you choose me."

". . . Listen to what I'm saying here: there's no getting out of this damn hole. I'm right! And what's more, you know I'm right. Look, come another war, we ain't the ones who're going to suffer, uh-huh. And don't be such a damn jackass! You know who tends to lose if there's another war? *They* do; they got more to lose, too. Hell, we're already down in the pits. It could be, now, it just might, that we'll do right well if another war does come along."

". . . And you know what I went and did? Well, I walked in to town to buy myself a new hammer. Yeah; I was going to be ready to go to work just as soon as that carpenter or whatever he was, came in to teach us something. And you know what people are now saying? They're saying that the preacher, as soon as he heard about his wife and that other guy, that he went into that house of theirs, grabbed himself an ax, and broke every stitch and piece of furniture they had there. And then he piled everything outside, and once he'd done that, he set the damn thing on fire. Watched it, too; stood there watching that fire until all there was left was the ashes . . ."

"No, I don't see how my husband's going to be able to

work out in the sun anymore. And when we told the grower that my husband had been beat down by the sun, know what he did then? He shrugged. Walked away. That man had other things on his mind. Rain, for one; the crop, for another. So, it was the rain and the crop he was on about. And listen to this: his wife came down with a cancer and was operated on. And even that didn't worry him as much as the crop. So, you tell me how much he cared when we told him about my man, my husband."

". . . No such thing. There's no such thing as a devil or anything like it, either. The only devil around here is Don Rayos—Old Man Lightning—and that's because he dresses with that cape and he wears those horns during the Christmas plays. Devil? What devil you talking about?"

". . . You blind? What the hell's wrong with you? We almost hit that damn truck! Couldn't you see it? 'Ta hell's wrong with you?"

". . . That youngish teacher, she started to cry. Why'd she cry for? For that Mexican kid? When they took him away?"

"Young and inexperienced, not like those in Texas; back home, they're old and born with a stick in their hands ready to whack you one if you lost your place on the reading. And if you lose it, it's bend over and whack! No less than five licks, yeah."

122

". . . And you think that's why they broke up? It's hard to believe, that's all. Hard to believe they broke up that fast."

". . . It was a hot flame and then once the clothing catches fire, that's it, you can just forget it."

"Yeah, I guess. You remember that other family? Burned up around Christmas time, I think it was. They burned up in their sleep. And then the firemen cried like babies when they carried the little bodies out. Those hot flames had rendered the kids' fatty tissue, and this splattered all over and inside the firefighters' boots . . ."

". . . Free citizens! This is an important, nay, a glorious day for all of us. Eighteen-sixty-two it was, when the troops of the great Napoleon went down in defeat as they faced the brave Mexican forces who so gallantly . . . Well, that's the way I'd start all my speeches, my oratory. And the term *free citizens*, sovereign people, see?, that was something I always used. A-course, I was younger then, m'boy, but then this stroke came and there went my legs, my boy . . . And it's even affected my thinking, too . . . I can't seem to remember what else I'd say to the people in those days . . . And then? Well, the 1910 Revolution came rumbling through and our side lost; we lost at the end, but losing is the same everywhere. Pancho Villa? Oh, he did all right for himself; he's one of the ones who came out ahead. Not me. I had to come to this side of the Rio Grande. But there's no one here who knows what I did over *there*. What it was I did during the Revolution. And now, I try to remember myself what it was I did, but I can't. Memory's all gone, boy. But let's leave that. Now, I want you to tell me what it is you really and truly want, more than anything else. At this time and moment, boy, at this time in your life, right now. What is it you really want?"

"... We came up with 50 pounds of copper wire yesterday. Enrique found himself one of those big magnets to locate metals with. Easier, see? People throw away a lot of stuff, but that magnet goes right to the iron metals. We do okay sometimes. But, most of the time, well, most of the time we come up empty; it's a waste of time. Can't even come up with enough to eat a snack somewhere. What are they paying for tin foil these days? Say, why don't you all come with us the next time we go out?"

"... That cold weather is coming on. We'll get us a hard freeze tonight. I bet it covers the ground. And the high flying cranes, you seen 'em? They're flying south about as fast as you'll ever see 'em ..."

"Sunday? There's a wedding on then, and I can tell you right now what they're going to feed us. *Cabrito en mole*. That good old roasted kid goat, and rice to go with it. A bed of rice, yeah. And then there's the dance, right? And how about that groom? Ha! Antsy as hell for night time to come, ha!"

"... Did you say fright? I'll say we had one, Comadre. There we were, talking, watching the kids, when out of the blue, the lights go out. And dark? Hooo! And you know what else, Comadre? We didn't have a single, solitary candle anywhere in the house. But that didn't scare us as much as what happened next. That Juan of ours, and he can be such a little rat sometimes, he—and don't ask me how—but he shoved an orange seed up his nose. In that dark. Yes, he did. So he cried, and *how* he cried. And my husband? Well, all we had was matches, like I told you, and there he was lighting matches while we tried to get that seed out. He'd light one, he'd light two, and like that."

"Well, what was it happened that night anyway? We heard the whole town was dark, that right?"

". . . The way I hear it, Doña Amada's boy was found by the irrigation canal, but Don Tiburcio's boy, he burned right inside that van. Now I don't really know, but I heard Don Jesús is going to be sued plenty over this thing; him and his van and carrying people while that back door was locked from the outside. It trapped them, see? As for Don Tiburcio's boy, well, some people went inside the van to get the boy out. The people they tried to stretch the body out to take him outside, but when they tried to stretch him, a leg dropped off . . ."

". . . The picture guys? Nah, they don't show up here anymore. And they won't, not after Don Mateo gave 'em what for."

". . . Ma? Yeah, she almost went out of her mind for a while there. And then she'd cry up a storm every time she'd talk about what happened to her when she went downtown that time . . ."

(I wish I could see all those good people at once, together, at the same time. And then, if my arms were long
enough, I'd reach out to embrace 'em all. Give 'em a warm
hug. And I wish I could talk with them again; see them all
here, together; the only way I could—can—do that is in a
dream. Somehow.)

It's a good place, under this house. I can think about
anything I want to. But you have to go off by yourself to do
that, to be alone. And then, when you do that, you can get all
the people together. Gather them in one place, in one thought.
And I needed to get away. Needed to hide, be off by
myself to learn, know, to understand, finally. From here on
out, all I've got to do is to come here, in the dark, and then I
can go back in time and think about those fine people. But
there's never enough time, it seems. I've so much to think
about and so little time. I think that today's the one day I
wanted to remember all of last year. But that's only last year,
and what I want, need to do, is to come back to this place, to
remember all the other years . . .

A child's cry and then a painful sensation down the leg.
Rocks! They're throwing rocks at me. Why?

"Mamma, Mamma, there's some old guy there, under

the house. Come quick, Mamma. Hurry, will you? It's some old man down there . . . some old guy."

"Where did you say? Where is he? Oh . . . Here, I'll go get some long sticks, switches; and tell you what: you go get Doña Luz's dog. Go!"

Looking up in the clear daylight, he could see eyes looking at him. Then it got darker under the house as more people blocked out the daylight; and the kids kept throwing rocks at him, and then they brought the dog and it started barking. And here was this woman trying to switch him, trying to get him.

"Who is it down there?"

In the end he had to get out; nothing else he could do. Why, that's no old man at all, they said. They knew him. Sure they did.

And he walked away, slowly. As he did so, he heard this old lady say: 'What a family . . . and such a shame, too. First their ma, and now this boy of theirs. Maybe he's going crazy, too. Got a screw loose somewhere, rattling around in that head of his. He's . . . he's lost some years, some time. Know what I mean?'

But he wasn't crazy. He smiled and pointed toward home with head held high through that chuck-hole ridden street he lived on. And he was happy; oh, he'd heard that woman say those things, but so what? What did she know?

He hadn't lost a *thing*. A year? He hadn't even lost a

day! He'd found! Re-found, recovered, you might say, and as a result he could connect things, weld them together.

Yes, to connect things, to make relationships, and to discover patterns: this goes with this, and that with that over there, and this with this, and all with all . . . That's what it was all about. And that was a lot. It was everything.

And he became happier still over this find, this personal discovery of his. First thing he did once he was home was to head straight for that shade tree of theirs. Up he went, shinnying up he went, and when he stopped, he looked some distance away, and there was that old, familiar palm tree.

Was there someone there, in that old palm tree, he thought to himself? It seemed as if there were. He kept this eyes on the palm tree. And it seemed he could make out someone over there, waving at him. Yes. Saw him raise his arm, waving to him, waving to let him know that he knew he was *there*.